# A
# Thug's
# Life

## Thomas Long

**Urban Books**
**6 Vanderbilt Parkway**
**Dix hills, NY 11746**

*Urban Books*
*6 Vanderbilt Parkway*
*Dix hills, NY 11746*

© Copyright 2004 Thomas Long

ISBN 0-9747025-3-6

First printing December 2004

10 9 8 7 6 5 4 3 2 1

Printed in Canada

# Dedication

This book is dedicated to all the fallen soldiers in the game, and food for thought for all those who are still caught up in the mix: Don't let the streets take your mind, body, and soul. It gets greater later, so give life a chance. It's much better on the other side.

# Acknowledgments

*Thank-yous go out to the following:*

The Most High, my Creator, for giving me the creativity and insight to be able to write and try to make a difference with my work in this crazy world; to my friends and family for your support; to all my "critics" who I allowed to read my manuscript in its raw form (it's too many to name, but you know who U R!), I appreciate your blunt honesty; Kelli Robinson and Tracey Hemphill- y'all some crazy chicks!; to my big homie Richard Holland (it's almost time, cat!), thanks for keeping me focused; JL White (Officer Friendly), a true friend to the end; Todd Alexander and the whole Alexander family, I feel your loss and keep you in my prayers; D. Pointer and T. Pointer, my homies from way back, and always will be; the staff at ARCC, I'll still make it to work on time (wink!, wink!); Fatima, the shy, innocent one; to my DC fam: Anthony and everybody at Imagine U Unique, I appreciate your hospitality every time I was in your neck of the woods; Harry Singleton , what's up, man!; my barber and ace boon coon, Paul Fenwick, steel sharpens steel (only U know what I mean); my man T- where da party at?; Twon, let's take it back to 2000! Sean Houston and Barry Heigh, my Woodlawn homies; Sekou Steeple, meet me down in Rio, kid!; The Smith brothers, diamonds in the rough, it's time for y'all to shine; D. Chase, keep striving Black man!; Sean Augustus, it's always love; Robert M. Jackson, U still my dawg, no matter what!; all my homies from Rogers Ave: Shawn Brewton, David Finch, Yomi, Neal, Darrell, Basil, Steven Ivy, the Bolling family, D. Woodson, T. Phillips, and everybody else's name that I can't recall at this time (blame it on all them late nights at the computer that my mind is on freeze!); to the streets of Baltimore City, I promise to represent with pride and to bring nothing but the rawest, uncut joints to let the world know that the game is real in B'more.

*Much love to the following friends who I've made in the field:*

Shannon Holmes- you showed a cat love from day one and schooled me on a few things, quiet is kept. It's dinner on me next time you in B'more!; Vickie Stringer, thanks for lettin' me shine in "The Game"; Marlon Green, let's get this money, man! MSU forever; Kwan (young Donald Goines), I see big things in your future, kid!; Alex Hairston, B'more is in here! I'ma see you on the bestseller's list in a minute; B. Lawson Thornton, U still my favorite East River girl; Brenda Thomas, U R just that woman. No more needs to be said; K. Elliott, your time is right around the corner, so keep grindin' down there in the Dirty South!; Gregory Simpson, keep pumpin' out them classics in the ATL; Miss Tiffany Womble, keep sh@* liquid!; my agents, Marc Gerald and Earl Cox, I look forward to a long and prosperous relationship with y'all dudes (Marc, I'm still hating that you got all that sunshine out in Cali (lol)); Mel Brooks- a poet extraordinaire and mack from way, way back (U got the best hand!); Notre Maison, Jackie, your poetry spot is a reflection of you: stylish, smooth, and a cool place to kick it!; my street vendors: Massamba in NY and Carvellas in DC, good looking out; all the other writers in the Urban Books family, I wish every one of y'all much success; Urban Books Executive Assistant Robilyn Heath, thanks for setting up my tour; Martha Weber, thank you for putting the final touches on my work; last, but most important, Carl Weber, the opportunity that you're giving me—I can't really put it into words how grateful I am. All I can say is that my word is my bond that I'ma keep delivering the hot manuscripts. You're da best, man! That's from da heart.

**--T. Long**

# A Thug's Life

By Thomas Long

I come alive when the soles of my Nike Airs
touch down on the concrete.
It's time to get that money,
I've got the wind beneath my feet.

No fear in my heart,
ice water in my veins.
Walking through the shadows of darkness,
I feel no pain.

This game is all that I live for,
yet my conscience calls out for so much more.
No friends, only potential enemies,
my mind is constantly at war.

Looking over my shoulder,
never knowing what to expect.
Relying on this piece of steel, tucked in my dip,
to keep these haters in check.

The women, they love my gangsta,
when they hear my name ringing on the block.
It's amazing what some people will do,
scheming and plotting to take my spot.

I'm getting tired of the rat race,

living life at a fast pace.
I need to find a way out,
before I wind up catching a case.

Niggas might not understand,
but it's time for me to be my own man.
My life is passing me by,
I gotta come up with a plan.

I'm willing to accept all of the consequences,
letting my actions speak louder than words.
Seeing the pain in my mother's eyes,
a cold feeling she surely doesn't deserve.

I'm filled with the worst self-hatred,
resenting the man that I've become.
The guilt keeps me humble,
because I understand that what is done is done.

In my heart, I'm looking for a change,
but my soul is consumed by all the scars.
On my knees, I pray to God,
hoping that he frees me from these mental bars.

**This Is A Thug's Life**

# 1
# One of Dem Nights

"That's right, girl. Just back that ass up," I said to Jaré as we got ready to engage in another one of our raunchy episodes in the bedroom.

She positioned herself with her backside facing toward me as I placed all ten inches of my manhood inside her. She sighed in ecstasy in response to the pain that would soon bring her the most exhilarating pleasure. I thrust in and out of her, enjoying every stroke as my dick became engulfed in the moisture of her oval office. She grabbed the headboard with both hands to keep her balance as the pace of my thrusts increased. She started grinding her hips in sync with mine as we listened to the sounds of Jahiem's *Ghetto Love* CD blasting out of the stereo. I knew she was loving how a playa was doin' the damn thing.

"Don't stop, papi. You know I love that shit!" That's what Jaré screamed as I continued to pound her insides like a brotha getting his first piece of ass after a five year bid in the pen. I couldn't even front—this girl had some seriously good punany.

After about a half hour of hittin' it doggy style, I turned her over and laid her on her back so I could look into her enticing, hazel eyes and caramel complexion as I waxed that ass missionary style. She submissively wrapped her long, shapely legs around my waist as I entered her, and we got down to the business at hand. She placed her hands behind my neck and cradled my head as she pulled me toward her, asking me to suck on her invitingly erect nipples. I willingly obliged as her screams of passion became louder and louder in my ear.

"You know this pussy belongs to you, papi. You can have it anytime you want it."

Hearing those words only excited me more and increased my desire to please her in every way that night. She started saying something in Spanish, making me go wild. I didn't know what she was saying, but it sure sounded like music to my ears. I continued to enjoy the good feeling of my voyage inside her love canal until she playfully whispered into my ear that she wanted to get on top and ride me. As she mounted my love muscle, which was still up to the task after about an hour of intense lovemaking, she rode me like she was a veteran cowgirl on her prized stallion. There was no doubt in my mind that Jaré was the one. The one for the night, at least.

She ran her fingers seductively through her hair as she did a slow grind on top of me. The sultry sounds of Sade played in the background. As she leaned down toward me, Jaré nibbled on my ear and said all kinds of nasty shit to turn me on.

"I want you to come inside of me, papi," she said as her pelvic gyrations became more intense. I knew she was about to cum, and I was ready to do the same.

I grabbed her waist tightly and she held the sheets as we both braced ourselves for what was coming next.

"I'm coming, Dayvon! I'm coming! Ohhhh shit!" she yelled as she reached her climax.

"I'm coming too, baby. Damn, this pussy is good!" I said as I exploded like a volcano inside of her. She lay on my chest, still moving her hips on top of my deflating manhood. I pulled her toward me and kissed her gently on her forehead to let her know she handled her business tonight. Wrapped up in the wrinkled sheets was how we fell asleep.

Jaré was the type of sistah with a body that just don't quit—the type that was made to be in *Black Tail* magazine. She stood about 5 feet 7 inches and 145 pounds, with long, dark brown, wavy hair that hung down to the middle of her back. Her hair texture could be attributed to her Black/Puerto Rican mixed heritage. She had a slim waist, six pack of abs, and an ass that poked out so much that a playa could set a glass of Cristal on it like it was a dinner table. Her breasts weren't necessarily large, but they were big enough for a brother to get more than a mouthful. Plus, she had a pair of deep, dark chocolate nipples that always managed to stay at attention. I'd had no choice but to make her the one I chose that night over three years earlier when me and my boy, Ty, were at The Cathouse gentlemen's lounge doing our usual Friday night "community service."

It was our ritual on Fridays to spend some of our hard-earned money looking at some fine-ass ghetto sistahs in thongs. After all, why not? We were young, black, getting money, and just living life to the fullest extent. We figured we might as well have a little fun. We had the streets locked down, and there appeared to be no end to our cash flow.

On this particular night, the DJ was blasting "How Do U Want It," one of my favorite Tupac joints, and the ladies were looking sexy as hell in their exotic outfits. We sat in our usual section at the bar. I was sipping on a RumRunner with just the right mix of Bacardi 151 to take the edge off the blunt Ty and I had just smoked in the parking lot. I was definitely in my own zone at that point.

That was when I spotted Jaré at the bar all alone, waiting for a young playa like myself to ask to buy her a drink. She had on a candy apple red thong and a form fitting baby T-shirt that read *Ass 2 Go* on the front. It barely covered her breasts. I had already seen her dance earlier in the night, so I knew she was working with something from head to toe. My man, Ray, who was a bouncer at the club, put me down and let me know she was new to the spot and had just come to town from Brooklyn, up in New York City. That was just what I was looking for—some fresh meat—because I was a hungry predator on the prowl.

When I made my move to approach her, I had already caught a glimpse of her checking me out. I guess she was impressed with the bling from all the ice dangling from my wrist and pinky finger. Or maybe she'd gotten a whiff of my 212 cologne when I walked by her coming into the club. Either way, after we made our introductions, I obliged her and agreed to buy her a drink and follow her to the VIP lounge for a lap dance. The VIP room was where only the cats with a little scrilla could go with a young lady, maybe get a little something extra if she was down for it.

As she guided me to the VIP lounge, I got a glimpse of that ass, and needless to say, I was mesmerized by how firm and round it was. Once we got in the room, she sat me on the plush couch and gave me a lap dance I will never forget. I'd been kickin' it with her ever since. Still, even though I saw her on a regular basis, she knew she wasn't my girl and I wasn't her man. We had an open relationship and enjoyed hanging out whenever we both had free time. Our arrangement was just perfect for me.

On the real tip, though, Jaré was a good girl who just had a few bad breaks in life. She grew up in Marcy projects in Brooklyn with her moms and two little sisters. She never knew her pops, because he died when she was two years old. Her moms told her he got killed over a craps game. Times were hard for her and her family growing up; it was a struggle just to survive. Just like so many other young, black females from the hood, she got involved with a young hustler named Malik and got pregnant when she was sixteen. Her moms wasn't having it with another mouth to feed on her low wage job, so Jaré wound up moving in with Malik after their son, little Malik was born. She was actually living ghetto fabulous, enjoying the fruits of being a hustler's wifey until Malik got knocked on a drug charge and had to do a ten-year bid.

Forced to survive on her own, she got turned on to the stripping game by her girlfriend, Sasha, a sure 'nuff hoodrat, down to run game on any young hustler for his loot. She had light brown skin with a short, Halle Berry type of hairstyle that complemented her dark brown eyes and high cheekbones. She stood about 5 feet 6 inches tall and had a set of legs that would make Tina Turner stop and stare in awe. It was nothing for her to make between five hundred and a thousand dollars a night at The Funkbox just for letting a man get his feel on and fantasize about fuckin' her.

Jaré saw the kind of loot Sasha was making and she was all too with it to make some ends herself, to take care of her and little Malik while her man was locked down. She only had to work three nights a week to make enough money to take care of all her material needs and wants. You could say she had it made. She danced at The Funkbox for about two years before Sasha heard about a club called The Cathouse in Baltimore where they could make twice as much loot and not have to work as hard for tips. After pondering on it for a minute, they decided to move to Baltimore, and had been there ever since.

Jaré wasn't really worried about her relationship with big Malik when she decided to relocate, because her visits to the prison had dwindled from once a week to once in a while. Over time, she had basically fallen out of love with Malik and made it clear it was over between them. She only continued to visit so her son could see his father. She wanted him to have a chance to get to know him, something she never got a chance to do with her own father. She promised she would continue to bring his son to see him after she moved.

When she moved to Baltimore, Jaré enrolled in college and was one year away from getting her bachelor degree in accounting at Morgan State University. That was one of the things I liked about her; she didn't fit the stereotypical image of a stripper who planned to keep stripping until she was a senior citizen. She was realistic and used the money she made from dancing to pay for school so one day she could get a better job to take care of herself and little Malik.

Aside from her beauty, the girl also had brains and a down to earth personality. She wasn't like most chicks who were as fine as she was but had their heads all up in the clouds. You know, the ones who turn their noses up to a brotha when he just speaks to them. My shorty had seen struggle in her life and she was from the hood, so that stuck-up mentality never grew on her.

If I were into relationships, she would definitely be a front runner to be the one I settled down with for the long haul. However, given my hectic lifestyle out in these streets, I knew falling in love was not in the plans for me. That just wasn't happening. I was having too much fun juggling the women in my life.

*Ring. Ring. Ring.*

"Hello."

"We have a collect call from Tyrone Adams at Roxbury Correctional Institute. Will you accept the charges?" said the operator's recorded voice on the other end of the line.

"Yeah." *Why the fuck did he have to call so early? Shit!* I thought.

It was my man Ty calling to make sure I was coming up for my visit that day.

"What's up, fool? Get your ass out that bed and up here to see me now. I know you're probably buried up under a piece of pussy up in there," Ty said, laughing his ass off.

"Damn, nigga, it's eight o'clock in the damn morning on a Saturday. Shouldn't you be up in your cell jerking off right now?" I shot back, knowing I was gonna piss him off.

"Are you coming up here or what?" Ty asked, ignoring my comment.

"Yeah, I'll be there around eleven-thirty. Hold your horses, fool," I answered.

"I was just checking, seeing how you forgot about a brother the last time, ya know. If I ain't know no better, I would think you was slippin' out there," Ty said in a half-joking manner. He was talking about two weeks ago when I missed coming up to see him because I stayed overnight in Delaware with Jaré after we spent the day gambling at Delaware Park.

"Whatever, man. I'ma see your ass in a few," I said. I was ready to hang up the phone and get back to looking at the fine piece of ass lying next to me.

"A'ight. Peace," Ty said.

"I'm out," I replied and hung up the phone.

By time, Jaré had woken up and looked over at me with her sexy-ass self. I couldn't help but blush because this girl had it going on in all ways. She would make a good wifey for some man one day.

"So, you going out to Hagerstown to see your boy?" she asked in a devilish tone.

"Yeah, I gotta get up in a few to take a shower and get dressed," I replied.

"Cool, but before you get up to take care of that business, I got some unfinished business for you to take care of down here," she said, gesturing beneath the covers.

"Want for nothing, mami, 'cause I got you," I replied as I threw the covers to the side. It was breakfast time, and I guess a large helping of some tasty chocha was what I needed to start my day. With that being said, I made my way down between her thighs and massaged her eagerly waiting clit with my tongue until she came all over my face.

"Thank you, papi. I needed that for real. I need to talk to you about something when you get back in town," she said as she gasped for air. I nodded to acknowledge what she had said to me, but I had no clue what she wanted to talk to me about. I would later learn I was about to make a decision that would change my life forever.

# 2
# If He Only Knew

*Damn, this nigga is fine.*

That's what I was thinking as I watched Dayvon get dressed. Dayvon kept his hair cut close, near bald, and his sexy, thin beard made him the image of perfection in my eyes. Just watching his chiseled, 6-foot 2-inch, deep, dark chocolate naked frame as he made his way to the bathroom to take a shower made me want to jump his bones. Physically, he was built like Ray Lewis from the Ravens and he had a tight pair of buns I just loved grabbing whenever he was putting his thing down inside of me. He had a tattoo of a panther on his left arm and one that spelled out the name of his crew, *Dogs For Life*, on his right arm. The words *Built 4 War* were scrawled across his shoulders, and the angel wings underneath them moved every time his muscles flexed. I just loved a thug nigga with tats all over his body. It drove me wild. This was my husband to be, no doubt!

I watched him get dressed and noticed the care this brotha took in making himself look fly from head to toe. His gear had to be matching from the pants and shirt he chose all the way down to his shoes. That's why when I saw him slide into his neatly pressed Rocawear denim pants with the shirt to match then put on his butter Tims, I knew he meant business when he stepped out into the streets. His confident attitude only added to his sex appeal. He knew he was the man.

I ain't gonna front, though, because before I met Dayvon, I had a totally different perception of Baltimore men coming from up north. I thought all Baltimore men were wack dressers and talked with a country accent that just turned me the hell off. I remember when I used to make those summer trips down here to see my Aunt Fran in East Baltimore. My older cousin, Chanel, used to take me out with her sometimes to show me the city when I was like fourteen or fifteen years old. I was kinda built for my age, so it was only natural I attracted a lot of attention from the older guys. The problem was I just wasn't feeling any of the guys Chanel tried to introduce me to. They all seemed to be trying to imitate New York niggas and didn't have any style of their own. Needless to say, fast-forward a few years, that all changed when Mr. Dayvon Freeman walked into my life.

Ever since Malik and I broke up before I left New York, I hadn't really been dating too much. I just wasn't in the mood for it in my life at the time. Plus, work, school, and my little man kept me plenty busy. Guys down at The Cathouse would always try to date me outside the club, but I had a rule I always kept in the front of my mind at work: Never take any of these sorry sleazeballs home with you, 'cause they ain't no damn good. Get the cash, but I sure ain't kickin' them out no ass. That was the golden rule Sasha and I tried to live by. I say *tried* because Sasha had developed a thing for money so bad she would do just about anything if the price was right. And I do mean anything.

She was my girl and all, but keeping it real, she acted like I didn't know she was fucking those young hustlers when she would do those private shows outside of the club. I ain't no genius or nothing, but I knew damn well that she was spreading them cheeks the way they all hovered over her at the club. Ain't that much lap dancing in the world. Plus, I knew she was a certified freak ever since that night she tried to come on to me.

It was one of them nights when I got a little too drunk at the club and couldn't drive home, so I decided to stay over at her place for the night. I'll admit I was tipsy as hell, but not too drunk to know when someone was trying to take advantage of me. I remember her asking to help me get out of my clothes, then wanting me to sleep in the bed with her.

Too drunk to argue, I agreed and laid my lush ass down to sleep. Well, in the middle of the night I felt Sasha's hands rubbing all over my body. At first I thought it was a dream, until I felt her tongue inside my ear. I instantly jumped up in shock and let her know I don't get down like that. I'm strictly dickly, no doubt about it. She apologized and we agreed to never speak on the subject again.

So, other than Sasha's attempt to sex me, I hadn't been in bed with anyone in what felt like forever. That's why I was feeling a little lonely and in need of some male company on the night I met Dayvon. It had been almost eight months since I had some sex, and I was definitely in the mood. When his fine ass walked over to me and asked to buy me a drink, all my rules went out the window. I had to have him that night. This man had a set of lips on him like L.L. Cool J that just said he loved to eat pussy. His cute smile and charming personality didn't hurt either. He didn't seem to be like most of the other hustlers who came to the club. He had his own style, and I was definitely feeling it.

When I took him back into the VIP room that night, I just knew I was going home with him. I made sure I gave him a lap dance that would get him as horny as I was for him. I teased, licked, and massaged every inch of him that I could. We both got so hot and heated we couldn't wait to get out of that club and back to his place to finish what we had started. Mr. Freeman did not disappoint me that night.

Besides being a pipe laying fool in the bed, Dayvon knew how to treat a lady. It was nothing for him to take me shopping or out to dinner and the movies. Going deeper than that, sometimes he even cooked for me when I stayed over at his crib. This man could really burn in the kitchen. Ain't many brothers out here today who treat a girl that way and have some class about themselves. Most men I meet don't even want to take you out. They think a girl is supposed to be content coming back to the crib, getting drunk, and fuckin' all night. Not me. A chicken head I would never be.

Even my son had taken a liking to Dayvon. Whenever he came over to visit, they would stay up for hours playing video games. Dayvon called him his li'l man. He had no problem taking Malik out with him when he cruised around town in his Lexus LS430. He'd kinda become like a father to my son since big Malik wasn't around to raise him.

The way Dayvon was with my son, it felt like we were a family. I couldn't admit that to him, though. We had agreed we would have an open relationship with no strings attached. Only problem was I was starting to get a little tired of our current arrangement. I wanted him to be my man, not just some part-time lover.

I don't know why guys put themselves in this position all the time, doing all the things a man is supposed to do for his woman, but then don't wanna commit to a real relationship. You would think they'd be smart enough to realize when a woman agrees to an open relationship situation and she's feeling you, all she's really doing is just buying time, hoping you change your mind and give her the commitment she wants from you. Damn them for spoiling us and not expecting us to fall in love.

After I got a few hours of rest to recoup from the previous night's romp with Dayvon, I got up to clean my place a bit. It was a far cry from the two-bedroom death trap I shared up in Brooklyn with my moms and two sisters. This was a nice, spacious, two-bedroom condo for me and my li'l man, situated in an upscale community outside the city. It was adorned with all of the finest amenities, from my imported European furniture to my 55-inch projection screen TV in the living room. Some things I bought for myself; the rest Dayvon got for me when he was feeling generous, which was most of the time. I must say I had made out pretty good for a girl from the projects in Brooklyn.

After I finished cleaning up, I decided to study a bit for an exam I had coming up next week. School was kicking my ass, but the 3.2 GPA I had was gonna be worth it in the long run. I knew working in a strip club wasn't gonna last forever, so I had to have a good backup plan. I wasn't gonna be one of those 35-year-old chicks with sagging breasts, trying to dance on a pole when I ain't got no business doing so. I was determined to be successful, and with the right man in my life, that would just make the picture complete for me and Malik.

I had started to doze off from studying when the phone rang.

"Hello."

"What's up, girl? You ready for tonight?" Sasha asked, sounding hyper as hell.

"Yeah, I was sitting here tryin'a study. I'm still tired from kickin' it with Dayvon last night after the club," I said.

"Damn shame, your hot ass," she said sarcastically.

Sasha was jealous of my relationship with Dayvon and always made some kind of smart remark about us. With all of her scheming and plotting, she never found one cat—or several combined—who would treat her as well as Dayvon treated me.

"Whatever, girl. What time do you want me to pick you up?" I asked her.

"Around seven-thirty. I gotta get there early 'cause I'm doing something special tonight. I heard them cats from Roc-A-Fella Records are coming to the club tonight. You know that means mad tips," she said.

"Cool. Just make sure you're ready when I get there," I said.

"Okay, okay. Oh, one more thing. Have you told your little *boyfriend* about your surprise?" she asked.

"No, not yet, but I will when he comes back in town from seeing Ty," I replied.

"Yeah, then you can see if he's really real with all this shit he's been doing for you, or if he's phony like his boy was with me," she said.

You see, Sasha and Ty were messin' around before he got locked up. He wasn't really diggin' her that much and only wanted to fuck her a few times then dump her. Of course, Sasha had her own plans after she saw how much money he was holding. Ty was living with his son's mother, Gena, and he was just messing with Sasha for a piece of side ass. However, when Sasha found out about his child's mother, she was pissed. Sasha was not about to play second fiddle to no bitch.

One day, Sasha decided to confront Gena and wound up getting the ass whipping of her life. Gena was one of them big Amazon girls—about 6 feet tall— and she just looked like she could fight. Sasha wanted me to get involved, but shit, I didn't tell her to be messin' with some other chick's man. She was on her own. From that point on, Ty stopped messing with Sasha altogether, and she never got over it.

"Yeah, we'll see what happens when I tell him the news," I responded.

"See you when you get here," Sasha said.

"Peace," I replied and hung up the phone.

Now Sasha had me wondering how in the hell I could break the news to Dayvon without him getting upset. I was two weeks late for my period and I just had a gut feeling something was wrong. I went to the doctor, and she confirmed my suspicion. I was excited as hell when she told me I was pregnant.

Dayvon and I usually used condoms in the beginning, but after we got familiar with each other, we stopped using them. He told me some nonsense that condoms don't feel natural and he wanted to feel the real thing when he was inside of me. Far be it for me to argue. I liked it raw, too. Just the thought of having all that big Mandingo dick inside of me was enough to make my panties moist. His dick fit inside my pussy like a hand inside a fresh leather glove—not too tight, but just right.

However he would handle the news when I told him, I convinced myself I would be prepared for his response. If he stuck around, then we could all be the family I wanted us to be. If he decided to bounce, which is what most young brothers do today, then I would be ready to raise my kids on my own still the same. You see, even though I liked to shop a lot, I was also smart enough to save up a hefty nest egg for a rainy day. I could stop working for at least a year and still pay all my bills with more than enough money to spare.

I pondered my situation a little longer, watching videos on BET until I dozed off to sleep on the couch. I needed my rest because I was out to make some major ends that night at the club. Talking to Mr. Freeman would have to wait for another day.

# 3
# Time For A Change

It was the perfect day to make the trip out to see my boy, Ty. It was springtime, the weather was warm, and the calmness of the air was relaxing for me. It was so warm I could roll the windows down on the whip to catch a nice breeze. This was a nice break for me, considering the amount of stress I'd been dealing with lately.

I popped in my *Better Dayz* CD to listen to some 2Pac as I cruised on the highway. The ride gave me a chance to do some thinking about my life and the choices I had made. I started thinking about the drama that had been going on in the streets lately and asked myself whether or not I wanted to end up being nothing more than another drug dealer who got lost in the game.

In the drug game, nobody gets away with making the amount of money we were taking down without suffering some losses. I had to admit we did have a nice, long, six-year run on top of the game, suffering only a few casualties of war. Lately, though, due to a lot of jealous cats snitching, I'd lost a few of my most loyal soldiers to either death or prison terms. It was getting to be too much for me.

Me and Ty controlled just about all of the drug trade in West Baltimore. Our DFL (Dogs For Life) crew consisted of over 200 street soldiers spread across the west side of town. Our drug strips included Garrison Boulevard and Liberty Heights, Park Heights and Belvedere, Pennsylvania and Gold Street, and all of Edmondson Village. We had four lieutenants appointed to deal with business on the street level in these major strongholds. Ty and I handled the politicking with our connections up north when it was time to get more product. We normally avoided touching any drugs personally, but everyone was clear as to who was running the show. On a bad week, we easily pulled in about $200,000 to split after paying all of our workers. On the first and fifteenth of the month, when the fiends got their welfare and SSI checks, our profits increased to at least three times as much. Shop was open bright and early, and we were right there, eager to get that money.

Since Ty got knocked on that bullshit conspiracy to distribute charge over two years ago and copped out to an eight-year bid, all the weight of running things had fallen on me. From all the late night calls when somebody from our crew got locked up and needed bail money to having to deal with beef from rival crews trying to move in on our territory, it was all starting to weigh on my nerves. This was what I was going to talk to Ty about, because I had decided it was time for me to make a change in my life.

Sometimes I would sit and ask myself how I came from a prestigious and well-respected family and wound up living the life of a drug kingpin. My father was a neurosurgeon at Johns Hopkins Hospital, and my mother was a high school principal. I grew up in the Randallstown area, far away from all the drama that takes place in the inner city. My older brother, Eric, my younger sister, Kiera, and I had all of the key ingredients in life to be successful. A stable, two-parent household with no financial struggles was rare to see in the black community. However, for some reason, I never fit into their middle class world. I guess you could say I was the black sheep of the family.

Eric graduated from the University of Maryland with honors and was an accountant for a Fortune 500 company in Atlanta. We didn't really keep in touch that much, but I did see him on occasion when I made my monthly trips down to Atlanta to see Cheri, my Georgia peach. He would usually go on and on, telling me about how I'd hurt my parents by embarrassing the family name and messing up my life. I could only take but so much of his tight, wannabe white ass before I was out the door.

Kiera, on the other hand, loved the ground I walked on and refused to give up on me no matter what everybody else said about me. She was in her second year at Coppin State College and planned to become an RN. She was my baby sis; we'd always been tight, and always would be 'til the end.

Anyway, it seemed as though my world had taken a 180-degree turn from the structured, suburban family environment I was raised in, and I couldn't figure out where I got off track. All I could do was retrace my steps to when I first met Ty and think about how we got started dealing. I met Ty when I was 13 years old and we used to play in the BNBL summer basketball tournament. My team, the Randallstown 76ers, used to play his team, the Park Heights Lakers, in the tournament champion-ship every summer. One year his team would win the championship, and the next year my team would win. We were each stars on our teams and both played the point guard position. Our battles on the court were legendary, kinda like watching Allen Iverson and Stephon Marbury go at it in the NBA, except we were much younger. Out of our intense competition, Ty and I managed to develop a mutual respect for each other and eventually become the best of friends.

Ty's family life was the direct opposite of mine. He grew up in the Belvedere Avenue and Park Heights section of the city, which was infamous for its drug activity. Both of his parents were long-time drug addicts. They were killed together, execution-style, over a drug beef when Ty was six years old. It happened right in front of him and definitely left its mark on his psyche. After his parents' death, he was taken in by his Aunt Sheryl and Uncle Will, who lived a block down from Ty's parents.

Will was his mother's brother and he was heavy into the drug game. He had the money, jewels, cars, and women that made him a local ghetto celebrity. He became a father figure to Ty and introduced him to the drug game at the age of ten. Ty started out on the block, hand-to-hand serving the fiends their daily fix of either heroin or crack cocaine. Will knew that because of his age, Ty would never have to do any time if he got arrested. Like a true general, he schooled Ty in the rules of the game and molded him into a bonafide street soldier.

Ty introduced me to the game after we had been hanging out together for about two years. I was convinced I wanted in after I met his uncle. Will seemed to be the coolest cat in the world. He had it going on in all ways. He was kinda short and slim, only about 5 feet 7 inches and 150 pounds, but his reputation in the streets earned him much respect throughout the city. I was awed by the props cats would give him whenever we cruised around with Will in his drop-top Benz. I never knew a 16-year-old could have so much fun.

Hanging with Will, Ty and I got to do and see a lot of things most kids our age never had a chance to do. Will would introduce us to older women who were eager to please any of our youthful sexual fantasies just because Will said so. He would take us shopping for new clothes and just show us how a balla was supposed to live. We could get into clubs on the strength of Will's name, even though we were underage. The excitement I got from hanging with them was a far cry from my boring life in the suburbs.

I was able to hide my lucrative profession as a drug dealer from my parents for a while. I always managed to find some kind of bullshit job to use as a front. I worked at FootLocker and Changes in Mondawmin Mall while I was in high school. That gave me an easy and convenient excuse for how I was able to afford all of the expensive designer clothes I was wearing. I told them I got a discount at all the stores for working in the mall.

My parents never approved of my friendship with Ty. They saw him as just a ghetto kid who would wind up getting me into trouble. My dad tried punishing me and forbidding me to hang out with Ty, but after I continuously defied his wishes, he conceded and accepted the fact I would never let him choose my friends. Plus, I still managed to get A's in school, so I guess he reasoned I hadn't strayed too far from his wholesome nest.

That all changed when I was almost seventeen and had just graduated from Randallstown High.

That was when I got arrested for the first and only time on a humble. I had just served somebody and walked down the block when Five-O swarmed on me like I was Saddam Hussein or something. Luckily, I didn't have any product or money on me, so I knew the charge wouldn't stick. They were just trying to harass me to get me to tell them who I was working for, but I was too sharp for their mind games.

What I hadn't planned on was the rude awakening when my Dad had to come to the precinct to pick me up. Since I was a juvenile, my parents had to be notified. Needless to say, my father cursed me out royally. I could see the shame in his eyes. I tried to tell him it was all a misunderstanding, but he wasn't hearing it. He had made up his mind if this was the lifestyle I wanted to lead then I would have to move out of his house. My mother agreed with him. At that point, I was forced to move out on my own and my relationship with my parents had been strained ever since.

When Will decided he was getting out of the drug game, he turned everything over to me and Ty. Will was from the old school when hustlers had some class and it wasn't all the gunplay, like what my generation has going on today. He reasoned it was time for him to retire since he had made enough money from hustling and had flipped it into legitimate businesses. He would live lavish for the rest of his life. Now I was starting to think Will's plan was the road I wanted to take for myself to get out of the game.

Hagerstown, Maryland was about an hour and some change from Baltimore. It wasn't a nice place for a brother to have to serve his time. So many of my homies, including Ty, had told me about the harsh treatment they received from the racist, redneck correctional officers out there. They told me about how the C.O.'s would wake them up in the middle of the night and just take turns pulling out a can of whip-ass on a brother if they felt he ever got out of line with one of them. I knew this wasn't a place where I was trying to be a resident anytime soon.

As I got closer to my destination, the vibration of my cell phone startled me.

"What's up, baby? Can a sistah get a chance to holla at a brotha, or what?"

I knew that pretty voice anywhere. It was Cheri, my sexy dimepiece down in Atlanta. I hadn't spoken to her in about two weeks, so I guess she was feeling neglected.

"Come on, now. You know I ain't got nothing but love for you, girl."

"I can't tell. You haven't returned any of my calls," she said in her most innocent voice.

"Things been kinda hectic up here. I'ma be down there next weekend to tighten you up just how you like it," I said.

"Yeah, we'll see that when it happens," she said. She was trying to make me feel guilty.

"I promise you, boo, I'ma make it up to you. Now, let me take care of some business, and I'ma holla at you when I'm done," I said, trying to get her off the phone.

"All right," she said.

We talked for about another five minutes so I could reassure her I would see her the following week. After I got her off the phone, I made my way to the gate of the prison and into the visiting room to see Ty.

Ty stood about six feet tall, medium build, with a light brown complexion. He had a scar on his left cheek from scuffling with a junkie who he had to beat down for stealing from us. Ty wasn't the most handsome brother, but his thug nature attracted more than enough women.

In our drug family, I was considered to be the brains of the operation and Ty was the muscle. Whenever we had to haggle over prices for some product, I was the negotiator. As for Ty, he was quick to put the murder game down when it was needed to let the competition know we were not to be fucked with. Only he really knew how many bodies he had unclaimed on the streets. If he didn't tell me, I never asked him about the rumors I had heard.

We embraced and gave each other a pound because it had been a minute since we had seen one another face to face. Ty and I were like brothers, even though we had no blood relationship. We had the kind of bond Eric and I could never share, because we just weren't cut from the same cloth.

Ty was waiting anxiously for me to fill him in on what was going on in the streets and how the money was flowing. As we talked, I told him how things were going down with the family and what was going on with me. I told him about who got knocked and who I had to kick out the crew for lunchin'. I told him about how Gena and his son were doing and, of course, I told him about my sexual escapades with the women in my life. Cats in jail loved to hear that shit; it gave them something to fantasize about when they got back to their cells at night.

After we joked and laughed for a while and I had brought him up to date on the current events, it was time for me to tell him the news that had been eating me up for the last few weeks. I couldn't wait any longer, so I decided to just say it straight up, pulling no punches.

"Yo, man, I've been doing a lot of thinking lately about getting outta the game for good," I said.

"What the fuck you talking about, man?" he asked with a confused, angry look on his face.

"I'm saying, yo, this game ain't gonna last forever. We done had a good run in this shit. I think it's about time we make that change like your uncle did," I said. I was hoping he would agree.

"My uncle is old, man. I'm twenty-six years old, full of life, and I'ma be thuggin' in this shit 'til the day I die. Besides, what else am I gonna do, go to college and be some bookworm and shit?"

From the expression on his face, I could see he was dead serious. Ty didn't see any reality besides being a hustla until they put him in the grave. It was all he knew and all he aspired to be.

I tried to reason with him. "Man, we done made enough money out here to live like kings for the rest of our lives without having to do this shit no more."

"Speak for yourself. Ain't no such thing as enough money for me. As quick as I spend it, I gotta go make some more."

He wasn't lying about his spending habits. Ty had a car for every day of the week and didn't believe in saving a penny. He was of the mentality you can't take it with you when you die, so you might as well spend it all. On the flip side, I invested my money wisely. I hired a Jewish attorney, Marty Weinstein, to launder my money and invest it in profitable stocks and bonds under a fictitious company name. I wanted to be sure that if I ever had to do time, I would have money waiting for me when I got out that the Feds couldn't touch under the RICO act.

"You need to check yourself, homey, 'cause ain't no way out of this shit except death. You forgot what DFL stands for?"

I stared in disbelief at his veiled threat. You see, when we first started the DFL crew, Ty and I had taken a blood oath that we would be in the drug game together for life. We vowed if either of us ever broke this oath, the penalty would be death. We were young at the time, and ignorant as hell to the changes life would throw our way. Back then, life was all peaches and cream with the money, women, and respect we got. Now that I was many years older and wiser, I saw the dead end road the streets really had to offer. I refused to be bound by a boyhood oath now that I was a grown-ass man, capable of making more responsible decisions.

"Look, Ty, I'ma keep things tight for you with our crew until you get out in six months. After that, I'm out," I said. I looked him dead in his eyes to let him know I was serious. I wasn't about to back down from my statement.

"Do what you feel, Day, but just know I ain't gonna forget this shit. I always knew you was a suburban nigga trying to be a thug," he said.

"Whatever, Ty. Fuck you. I'm bouncin' because you talking some crazy shit for real."

Those were my last words as I got up from the table and walked away from a dude who I thought was my brother. He started cursing at me loudly, making a scene for everybody to see. He was straight violating the code about handlin' family business out in public.

I tried to convince myself Ty hadn't become so caught up in this street life that he forgot the long history we shared. I knew Ty could be dangerous and capable of some sinister shit when he was angry. However, I was too smart to get caught slippin'.

Still buggin' off of what had just happened, I picked up my cell to call Cheri back. The phone rang three times before she answered.

"Hello." She sounded sexy as ever.

"What's up, boo? What you wearing right now?"

"Nothing but a thong and one of your T-shirts to keep me warm," she said.

"Damn, girl. I'm on my way down there tonight," I said in response.

"Yeah, right, Dayvon," she said with doubt in her voice.

"I'm serious, RiRi. I'm stressed out and need to get away for a minute," I told her.

"I got something to help you out with that stress, Daddy. What time are you coming?" she asked.

"I'm not sure yet. Let me check the flight schedule and hit you back to tell you what time to pick me up from the airport."

She agreed and I hung up the phone to call the airline to make my reservation. Then I called Cheri back and gave her the information so she could meet me at the airport. Lying up in the sunshine with a sexy sistah in a stress-free environment was just what I needed to take my mind off this nonsense I had to deal with. When I returned home, I knew it would be time to face the music after the fire I had just started.

# 4
# Welcome To Atlanta

The plane ride to Atlanta was so calm and relaxing I slept the whole trip. I would've kept on sleeping if it weren't for the fine-ass stewardess who woke me up. I had been flirting with her when I first boarded the flight and she must have liked it, because she slipped me her number on the DL when I was exiting the plane. She was one of them long-legged, big-breasted Italian broads, straight from Italy. They weren't like the Italian girls born here in America. Sicilian chicks were built like sistahs, for real! Her name was Isabella. I would definitely be holding on to her number for a rainy day when I might need some out of town ass or a place to lay low. Ain't nothing wrong with a little milk in my coffee every now and then.

Before I left for my trip, I made sure I left proper instructions with all of my crew as to how to handle business while I was gone, but I never told them where I was going. I knew Ty was still pissed at me after my visit, and there was no telling what kinda crazy shit his evil ass might cook up for me. He had called me two times before I left my house, but I didn't answer the phone. I wasn't in the right frame of mind to deal with his bullshit. I was hoping that after a little time to think, he might cool down and see things from my point of view. I was also playing it safe just in case he was trying to bring me some drama.

I left Pooh, who ran all of Edmondson Village for us, in charge of things, and made sure all of my other lieutenants were straight as far as product for a couple of weeks. All of our other lieutenants—Li'l Jay, Stink, and Ronnie-O—were leadership potential and kept their crews tight, but I chose Pooh to be in charge because he was the one who was most loyal to me. We had become tight from the time I first put him on with us when he was like thirteen years old.

His pops had left him and his family when he was two years old. He didn't have any males around him to look up to for guidance, so he turned to me. He was a smart kid and he knew growing up as the man of the house meant he would have to take care of his moms and sister. When he came to me one day on the strip and asked to get on, I couldn't tell shorty no after he told me how rough shit was at home.

Over time I became like a big brother to Pooh. I groomed him the same way Will had groomed Ty. He was a hustlin' li'l nigga, and that was why even though he was only eighteen, he was running his own crew now.

Pooh never forgot how much love I showed him or the trust I put in him. I knew I had Pooh's loyalty for life. He would kill a nigga with a quickness if I ever needed him to. You always need to keep soldiers like that around you in this game.

While I was sitting in the airport waiting for Cheri, I checked my messages at home and on my cell phone. Kiera had called and left me a message just to check on me. I would give her a call when I got to Cheri's house. There were a couple of messages from Jaré wondering where I was, ranting and raving about needing to see me. She would have to put that shit on freeze until I got back in town. The last message I heard was a pleasant, unexpected surprise from Nikki. Nikki was this fine Jamaican honey I had met at the club, Dreams, in D.C. a few months ago. She lived in P.G. County, and I'd been hittin' her off every now and then when I got a chance. She was definitely getting a call when I got back to B'more.

After I finished checking my messages, I shut off my cell phone. Cheri was gonna get my undivided attention while I was down here in the dirty South. I did, however, leave my other cell on. That line was strictly for business, just in case anybody from my crew needed to reach me. As I was gathering my luggage to go outside to wait for Cheri, I saw her walking through the lobby toward me. All eyes were on her as she strutted her sophisticated self through the terminal. This sistah knew she had it going on in all ways, and she loved the attention.

Cheri was nothing like Jaré. She had a unique vibe of her own. While Jaré was an around the way girl who was going to be successful through hard work, Cheri came from a rich, prestigious family, well known in the South. It was expected she would be successful. Her father was the president of MidSouth Bank and her mother was a well-respected attorney in the Atlanta area. She was the kind of girl my parents would have loved for me to get with, just because of her family's status.

Cheri had a good job as an advertising executive for some big company in downtown Atlanta. Many people might have wondered why she would want to deal with a dude from the streets like me. What they didn't understand was some of these upper class girls love to have a thug in their lives, tappin' that ass. That's where I came into the picture; I was only too eager to fill that need.

Cheri was petite, a little over 5 feet 2 inches, but she was living proof of the theory big things can come in small packages, because this girl had body for days. She looked something like a cross between Nia Long and Jada Pinkett with her sexy Cover Girl looks. She had an ass that made any pair of jeans look good. Every time I went somewhere with her, all the brothas were checking her out, but I knew them niggas wasn't gettin' no play. I had this pussy on lockdown, and Cheri made that clear to any cat that stepped to her.

I had met Cheri the year before when I was in Atlanta to check out the club scene. I had heard so much about the fine sistahs down there I decided to see for myself. We were both in Lennox Mall gettin' our shop on when I spotted her walking alone, carrying several large bags of clothes from all the expensive boutiques. That was when I stepped to her with my gentleman routine and offered to help carry the bags to her car. She fell for it hook, line, and sinker. Before the week was out, I had her in my starting lineup along with Jaré. I didn't have any commitment to any of my many concubines, so I was free to do whatever I wanted, whenever I wanted, and with whomever I wanted, with no questions asked. A lot of cats dream about puttin' down game like this, but I was really doin' it, and loving every minute of it.

Cheri greeted me with a big hug and a kiss on the lips to let me know how much I was missed. She had on some body-hugging jean shorts that showcased her hips and ass, and a midriff T-shirt that showed off her pierced navel. She had a tattoo of a tongue licking two cherries on her right thigh that made me just wanna bite her sexy ass right there in the airport.

"Damn, baby, you smell so good," she said with a lustful look in her eyes, like she wanted to lick me from head to toe the same way I wanted to do to her.

"Yeah, you smell like you taste good too, Ri," I said in return. I was talking about the cucumber melon scent she was wearing. My dick was about as hard as a brick when she rubbed her body up against mine. I was ready to fuck right then and there.

After we got back to her car and I put my bags in her trunk, she dropped the top on her BMW. We cruised down the highway en route to her Buckhead condo to chill. The weather was just like I liked it— not too hot and not too cold, a perfect spring night. We were listening to the smooth sounds of Heather Headley, and the coolness of the night breeze had me in a totally relaxed mood.

When we got back to her crib, it was as though I had stepped into a palace. Her place was laid out! The carpet was a rich, vanilla color and it was so plush it felt like I was walking on pillows. The living room was adorned with the finest Italian leather love seat and sofa set, and plenty of rare African sculptures and tribal masks that I know cost her some grip. Her bedroom was some exotic, freaky shit with mirrors on the ceiling right above her king-sized bed, so she could watch her sexual escapades. Cheri was a nasty-ass closet freak, and that's why I liked her so much. Li'l Kim ain't have nothing on her, trust me!

"You want something to drink, baby?" she asked as she turned on the wide screen TV in the living room.

"Yeah, let me get some Belvedere and cranberry juice," I said, watching her phat ass jiggle as she walked about the house. I was getting hornier by the minute.

She brought my drink over to me and poured herself a glass of White Zinfandel to sip on. We talked for a little while to catch up on things, and I was able to totally relax from the after effects of my flight. After about three or four drinks, we were both feeling drunk and horny as hell as we laid up against each other on the couch. That was when she got up and walked into the bedroom. What happened next was some shit that needed to be on the Playboy Channel for real.

I had started to doze off a bit when I heard Cheri call my name. I noticed she had turned out all the lights and lit scented candles all around the room. Cheri was standing in front of me wearing nothing but a black thong and a matching bra.

"Dayvon, why don't you come up outta them clothes and let me give you what I said I've been waiting to give you," she invited.

I couldn't even respond in words, but the way I was peeling my clothes off said more than enough. She walked over to the stereo and turned on the soulful melodies of Brian McKnight then started to dance seductively. By that time, I was ass naked on the couch, enjoying the show. She started to slowly, teasingly remove her bra. She knew watching her dance was turning me on.

When she made her way over to me, she got down between my legs, spread them, and grabbed my dick with both hands, licking slowly up and down my shaft. That shit felt so good. I almost lost my mind when she took all of me into her mouth and started sucking me off. I had to do all I could not to cum in her mouth.

After about thirty minutes of her getting my man to stand at full attention, I laid her on her stomach on the floor and licked her heavenly body from the back of her neck all the way down to her ankles. Her ass was perfectly round, and it tasted so delightful when I ran my tongue across both of her cheeks. She sighed loudly to let me know I was hitting the right spots. That was when I turned her over and did more of the same, devouring her pulsating nipples in my mouth one at a time. As I worked my way down, she started to giggle when my wet kisses reached her belly button.

I peeled off her thong with my teeth and she started to go wild as her body eagerly anticipated what was coming next. She knew I was about to go deep sea diving with my tongue. She raised her legs in the air to fully expose her neatly shaven crotch. I made my way back between her legs, placed them on my shoulders, and licked her clit in a swirling motion. She raised her body off the floor. Her screams got louder and more passionate by the minute. She came about three times before she pushed my face away with both hands.

"I want you inside of me *now*," she said with tears of joy in her eyes.

I granted her wish as I spread her thighs and inserted my dick inside her wet pussy, grinding in a slow, winding motion. She kept screaming for me to put it in deeper and deeper and not to stop as our pace of lovemaking increased. She came several times and I came also, but the night wasn't over yet. That was just round one, with much more to come.

As I lay on the floor to recuperate, Cheri went into the kitchen for a minute. She yelled for me to meet her in the bedroom. I went into the bedroom and lay across the bed. A few minutes later, she came into the room with a can of whipped cream in one hand and a bottle of Hershey's chocolate syrup in the other. For a good girl, she had mad tricks up her sleeve.

"What you planning to do with that shit?" I asked as though I didn't know.

"Have dessert . . . on you," she said provocatively.

She climbed onto the bed and got on top of me, then poured chocolate and sprayed whipped cream all over my chest. She licked every bit of it off me then sprayed whipped cream into my mouth. Our tongues curled around each other's in the kinkiest French kiss. When she made her way down to my dick, she covered it the same way she did my chest and sucked on it until all of the whipped cream and chocolate was gone. I was fully hard and ready to go back to work on her again. She climbed on top of my dick and rode it for about an hour, watching our lovemaking in the mirrors on the ceiling. Being able to see herself riding my dick turned her on even more. She jumped up and down on my love pole with more vigor. We both came ferociously, then made love several more times throughout the night until we passed out from exhaustion. This was the perfect beginning to my vacation, and I was looking forward to whatever Cheri had in store for me for the rest of my stay.

# 5
# The Set-Up

I was getting madder by the minute as I paced back and forth in my cell. Taking a drag off my cigarette, my mind was steady racing, wondering how I could have been so stupid to think me and Dayvon were like brothers all these years. When we got into this game, it was supposed to be for life, and we were always supposed to have each other's backs through thick and thin. After all the shit we'd been through, it got me heated that he would come up here to see me in jail to tell me he was getting outta the game. He wasn't even man enough to wait until I hit the streets to tell me. He had to have some shady shit up his sleeve.

I tried calling him several times after he walked outta the visiting room like a pussy, but he ain't pick up the phone, not once. Who the fuck did he think he was, not answering my calls? I let his ass get into the game, and I could surely take him the fuck out of it with a quickness. He knew how I got down, so I didn't know why he was even trying to pull some shit like this with me.

I got even madder when I found out from Li'l Jay that Dayvon had left town and didn't tell nobody where he was going. That got me wondering what the fuck he was really up to. Maybe the Feds had got to him and tried to get him to turn on me. Was he trying to set up shop somewhere else and not tell me about it? All types of crazy thoughts were going through my head. One way or another, I had to let this motherfucker know even though my ass was locked up, my arm was still strong out in them streets.

All my life, it seemed as though people had been telling me how much love they had for me and then, in the end, I wound up standing all alone. I can remember when I was a kid and my moms and pops used to tell me all the time they were gonna do right and stop getting high, but all that positive talk went in one ear and right out the other for me. As soon as one of their "get high" crew came around, it was the same old story. They would leave me, a little kid, in the house all alone while they were out all night chasing a blast of coke or some dope. Them junkie bastards cared more about their damn drugs than they did about their only child. Whenever they didn't have any money to get high, my moms would take her frustration out on me by whipping my ass until it was black and blue. My father was no better; he even tried to sell me to a dealer one time for some dope. That was why when them bastards got killed, deep down inside, I was happier than a motherfucker.

After I moved in with Will and Sheryl, I thought life would finally be different for me. I started thinking maybe I could have a normal life, a chance every kid should have. That idea changed real quick when Will had me out on the corner selling drugs for him at all hours of the night. The streets of Baltimore ain't no place for a 10-year-old kid to be hanging out, because he can get into all kinds of shit. I didn't really wanna do it back then, but I had no choice; Will and Sheryl were all the family I had left in this world. If selling drugs was what Will wanted me to do, then that was what I was gonna do.

Me and Sheryl never really got along. She was a nasty bitch with issues of her own. With all the fine women my uncle had, I always wondered why he messed with Sheryl. I mean, she was average looking at best. Later on, I realized it had nothing to do with her looks. It was because he could trust her with his money. He knew she would have his back if things got rough. All the other women he had only wanted him because of his reputation, but Sheryl had been there for him in the good and bad times. Every cat in this game needs at least one woman in his life who he can trust. Little did Will know how scandalous Sheryl really was.

I can remember back when I was about 12 years old. She used to come into my room when Will wasn't home and tell me to feel on her ass and suck on her saggy-ass titties. As time went on, it progressed to her making me eat her fishy-ass pussy and finger-fuck her. This 30-something-year-old bitch was getting her rocks off on a little kid who ain't know no better.

I couldn't tell Will. Sheryl said she would tell him I was lying and then Will would put me in a foster home. As sprung as Will was over her, I knew he probably would believe her, so I kept my mouth shut. Her sexual games with me went on for about two years before she finally left me the fuck alone. She was probably the reason why I still didn't know how to treat a woman the way she was supposed to be treated.

As time went on and I got better and better at the game, I decided to become the most ruthless and paid drug dealer Baltimore had ever seen. Shit, hustlin' was all I had in my life, and I knew it wouldn't betray me as long as I didn't betray the rules Will had taught me. Besides showing me how to make money, Will taught me never to take shit from nobody and never to pull a gun out on a cat unless I planned to use the motherfucker. He also taught me no snitching was allowed; the penalty was death. Finally, he told me never to fully trust anybody but myself, because friends can become the worst enemies when the heat is on. He said if I followed these rules, I could last as long in the game as he had. Up to this point, I had to admit he was right.

Now I was wondering if I had let Dayvon get

too close to me, and whether or not he was becoming my enemy. He knew things about me no one else knew, and I knew things about dirt he had done no one else knew. Having secrets about each other was a way to keep a tight bond between us, even when things got bad. However, in the back of my mind, I had always wondered how the police knew I was dirty that night I got locked up and caught this bit. After this stunt he was trying to pull, I was starting to think he might have set me up. If my hunch was right, then he was gonna pay for this shit with his life.

You see, when we had to go to New York to get some more coke, we usually sent Li'l Jay or Stink with a mule to pick the shit up after we had carried the money up there to pay our connect. However, that night we couldn't find Jay or Stink, so I'd decided to go get the shit myself. I was gonna be up there anyhow to check out this girl I had met on one of our other trips. In the back of my mind, I knew this was a bad idea, but I figured doing this run one time wouldn't hurt. It was a decision I would soon regret.

I got pulled over as soon as I crossed the state line back into Maryland. When they searched the car, they found my nine under the seat and the drugs stashed in the panels of the doors. Oddly enough, they seemed to know exactly where to look for everything. I knew I was royally fucked at that point. Luckily, I got a good attorney, and he plea-bargained my case down to eight years from the twenty they were trying to give me. I knew I would be home in three years or so with good time served. I couldn't complain much, because I got off pretty light given the circumstances.

Throughout all of the police interrogations, Dayvon's name never came up once, even though I knew the knockers knew he was my partner. That shit was really starting to fuck with me now. I was stuck up here in this hot-ass jail while that nigga was out there enjoying life. It made me wonder if he had let me take a fall so he could make all the money and then split town while I was gone. All kinds of crazy schemes were filling my head as I tried to imagine what he was thinking. Whatever Dayvon was up to, I had a way to handle the shit, and it wouldn't be pretty. Everybody else had betrayed me all my life, and he was gonna be the last motherfucker to cross me and to try to get away with it.

# 6
# Never Saw It Coming

April 26th was a day I looked forward to every year. That's because it's my birthday, and every year I celebrate it in style. Even though I had to work that night, I planned on making my twenty-fifth birthday something special for me. The first thing I planned to do was go to About Faces Day Spa in Towson to get a full body massage and be pampered, like the true diva I am. I was gonna use the gift certificate my moms had sent me for my birthday. After that, Sasha was gonna take me out to lunch at my favorite restaurant, Copelands, out in Columbia. Then I planned to do a little shopping with the money I had gotten from Dayvon through one of his boys, Pooh. Even though his ass hadn't been around to see me in over a week, at least he didn't forget my special day. In his own funny way, I knew he cared about me. I couldn't really be too mad at him for not returning my calls.

I'd been dealing with Dayvon for almost three years and I knew he had other women, but I really didn't care. When you think about it, all men cheat. It's just a part of their nature. It's my theory that they don't stop chasing women until they reach their mid-thirties and are finally ready to settle down. As long as he treated me right and showed me respect when he was with me, that was all I was concerned about. I knew that despite his faults, Dayvon was the man for me, and one day he would be all mine. The baby I was carrying was a guarantee I would have ties to him for the rest of his life. Them other chicks couldn't say that.

Lying around in the bed being lazy, I leaned over to check my clock. It was 9:30 a.m., time for me to get up and start my day. My spa appointment was at 11:00. I jumped out of bed and proceeded to the bathroom to take a shower. The warmth of the water against my flesh woke me up real quick as I lathered my body with jasmine scented shower gel. After I stepped out of the shower and dried myself with a towel, I stopped to observe my figure in the full-length mirror on the door of the walk-in closet. *Damn, I look good. Jennifer Lopez ain't got nothing on me in the ass department,* I thought.

I made my way inside the closet to find something to put on when I heard the phone ringing. It was my son calling me from my cousin, Chanel's house. He had spent the night there. He usually went over there to play with her kids on the weekends while I was at work.

"Happy birthday, Mommy. So, how old are you now?" he asked me.

"Mommy is twenty-five years old now, baby. Do you miss me?"

"A li'l bit. Dag, Mommy, you gettin' old as grandma," he said. He was laughing hysterically.

"Be quiet, boy. I'm coming to get you in the morning so we can spend the day together."

"Okay, Mommy. I love you."

"I love you too."

After I got off the phone with my baby, I went back into the closet to find something to wear that would make a statement about just how good I was feeling. I fumbled through my clothes for a few minutes before I found the perfect outfit. I had just bought these new fitted jeans with rhinestones on them. I figured I could hook them up with one of my Baby Phat tank tops for the perfect casual ensemble. I threw in my Prada sandals with the matching handbag and I was set. With that decision made, I got dressed and sprayed on my jasmine scented body mist, and then I was out the door.

My afternoon at the spa was so relaxing, and I just loved the service. The full body massage released all the tension in my muscles. My hair was done perfectly. My nails and feet were neatly manicured and painted with matching designs. I have to say, if I were a man and saw me that day, I woulda been trying to pick me up, without a doubt. This was definitely a good way to kick off my birthday on a positive note.

About thirty minutes after leaving the spa, I pulled up to Sasha's downtown apartment building and parked my Infiniti G35 in the parking lot. As I made my way to her apartment, I spotted one of her neighbors checking me out. He was a cutie, but he wasn't as fine as my Dayvon, so I just smiled and kept on walking. I made my way to the elevator to go up to Sasha's place. When I got to her floor, she was already standing in the hallway, about to get on the elevator to meet me downstairs.

"What's wrong with you? You ain't never on time when I come to get you," I said. Sasha was always late whenever we went somewhere together. She was definitely always on C.P.T.

"I don't know what you talking about. I'm always on time," she said. She was lying her ass off.

We both laughed as we got back on the elevator to go out to lunch.

We made our way into the restaurant right on time for our reservation. The hostess seated us at our table and gave us menus. For an appetizer, we split an order of Cajun steamed shrimp. As a main course, I ordered the baked catfish with garlic mashed potatoes and mixed vegetables. Sasha ordered crab cakes and Cajun fries. The food at Copelands was always excellent, and today was no different.

Feeling fat and kinda heavy after all that good food, walking in the mall was the perfect exercise to work off this extra weight. First we hit Towson Town Center and browsed around awhile before I found a few things I could add to my wardrobe. Next, we went to Owings Mills Mall, and it was pretty much the same thing, with me finding a couple of new outfits I could wear for the summer. I didn't want to buy too much stuff, because in a couple months I was gonna be carrying around a lot of extra weight from my pregnancy.

We did the mall thing for about three hours before I started getting tired and was ready for my midday power nap. I needed some rest because we had to work later on that night. With that in mind, I dropped Sasha off at her crib and made my way home to get some shuteye.

50 Cent was banging outta the speakers as I did my thing up on the stage. The DJ had announced it was my birthday, and all the guys were being generous with the tips. I was feeling extra sexy, so I gave them a show I knew had a couple of niggas ready to jerk off right there in the club. Sasha and I did a shower show that was totally off the chain, and them niggas just went crazy. We were the finest two girls in the club. As usual, all eyes were on us.

My regular customers bought me drinks all night long. By midnight, I was drunk as hell. I knew they were hoping I would get drunk enough that one of them would have a chance to get some play that night, but it wasn't gonna happen. This pussy belonged to Dayvon Freeman, and it was screaming his name for him to come and tear it up. Damn, I was horny as hell and I wished he was there.

The owner of the club, Kevin, bought me a big birthday cake with a picture of me dancing on a pole. He liked me and Sasha a lot because we worked hard and made sure his customers came back. Some of the other girls were jealous of us because we made the most money up in there. They would always give us evil stares and say all kinds of shit behind our backs, but they knew we were not to be fucked with. They didn't want no drama with two crazy-ass Brooklyn girls.

I must say that my birthday was definitely a good night to work. When I counted up all of my money at the end of the night, I had made close to two grand. That wasn't bad considering I only worked for four hours. That money would come in handy soon, because I knew I would have to stop dancing and drinking in the next month or so if I wanted to have a healthy baby. I wasn't gonna be one of those nasty-ass chicks I'd seen who be up on stage dancing in the late stages of pregnancy. That was just so disgusting to me. I had much more class than that.

It was almost two in the morning when the last of the customers were leaving the club. Sasha and I headed downstairs to take a shower and get dressed to leave. About thirty minutes later, we made our way to the front door to go home. Ray unlocked the door to let us out. We were both drunk as hell, but we'd had a lot of fun, without a doubt.

We walked about three blocks from the club to get to my car as we joked and laughed about some of the crazy dudes who were in the club. I took my keys out of my purse to unlock the doors and we got in the car to continue our conversation.

"Girl, did you see that wack-ass, played out Coogi set Eric had on? He must have got that joint out of some retired pimp's closet and shit," Sasha said and we both burst out laughing.

"Sasha, stop playin'. You know that's gonna be your baby's daddy one day. He bought you like ten drinks tonight, and you know what that means," I said. I kept laughing my ass off.

"Whatever, Ré. That nigga ain't never gonna get a chance to even smell this pussy," she said.

We were just having a good time getting our laugh on when Sasha pulled out a joint. I hadn't smoked weed in like a year, but I figured what the hell. It was my birthday. We blazed up the spliff. After about three puffs, I was high as hell, and so was Sasha. At that point, just about anything was funny to us.

"Damn, Sasha, this some good shit. I got the munchies now. Let's go get something to eat," I said. Sasha nodded in agreement and we decided to go to the IHOP out on Route 40 for breakfast.

As I was about to start the car, I saw a familiar black truck from the corner of my eye. It was speeding by and it caught me off guard. The next thing I remembered was a flashing light coming directly at me. The glass from the driver's side window shattered in my face. I heard Sasha screaming hysterically while a guy standing outside the car sent bullets through the passenger's side window. After that, I just blacked out.

# 7
# Smiling Faces Tell Lies

"Damn, we handled that shit, didn't we, yo?" I asked Stink.  We turned the corner onto the I-95 South exit.

"Yeah, them broads never knew what hit they asses, dog," Stink replied.

We had been following Jaré for the last few days to get her travel patterns down pat. While clocking her movements, we learned that when she went to work, she always parked in the same spot on a secluded side street. We figured it would be best to hit her there one night after she left the club, 'cause there were less likely to be any witnesses around.

It just so happened Sasha was with her the night we planned to carry out the order. She had to get it, too, because in the streets, witnesses will talk, but a dead body can't tell a motherfucker shit. It's business, never personal.

The plan had worked like clockwork. That night, we waited until the club closed and all of the customers had cleared out of the surrounding area. When we saw Jaré and Sasha walk outta the club about a half hour later, it was time for us to spring into action. We watched from the corner as they staggered toward the car. We could tell they were drunk as hell. When they got into the car, they didn't leave right away. They were sitting in there talking and laughing.

Stink got outta the Ford Explorer and crept up on the passenger's side of the car to take care of Sasha while I rode by and hit Jaré from the driver's side. Everything went smoothly. We both opened fire around the same time and riddled the car with bullets. There was blood splattered all over the car windows and windshield. The girls' bodies were slumped over in their seats. It was a job well done, if I do say so myself. After Stink got back in the truck, we sped off into the night.

As we drove, we were getting more amped up about the hit we had just carried out for Ty. He had given me the word he wanted Jaré killed to send a message to Dayvon. He told me Dayvon was a rat and needed to be dealt with.

Ty agreed to pay us ten grand each for the job. His plan was first to take away Dayvon's most cherished loved ones, so he would have to suffer pain like he never had before. Ty knew how much Dayvon cared about Jaré from all the things he did for her. Ty never knew him to treat another girl the way he treated Jaré. That being said, she had to go.

After Jaré was taken care of, he wanted us to kill Kiera, just to add more salt to his wounds. There was no doubt about how much Dayvon loved his baby sister, so she had to get it too.

Finally, when Ty got outta jail in a few months, he planned to kill Dayvon himself for the sweetest revenge. Ty was definitely a nasty, hateful motherfucker when someone got on his bad side. If he would do this to his right hand man, there was no telling what he would do to anybody else.

"Ain't no way in the world either one of them broads survived that shit, yo," Stink said. He was feeling confident the hit went down as planned.

"Shit, if they did, I'm down to do it again. I love catching bodies, nigga. Them was some fine bitches though, yo. We shoulda fucked them first and then killed they asses," I said, laughing my ass off.

"Yeah, I know Dayvon is gonna miss fucking that phat ass Jaré. That bitch had an ass like Beyoncé, for real," Stink said. He used his hands to demonstrate how her ass curved around into the perfect apple shape.

"We gotta ditch this truck now, yo. Let's get out to BWI airport so you can get your whip. Then you can follow me out to D.C.," I said.

We were gonna ditch the truck somewhere in southeast D.C. so if—or when—the police found the truck, it was as far away from Baltimore as possible. The truck was my weekend car, so I knew I wouldn't miss it but so much. I had reported it stolen earlier in the day so the police would never be able to tie it to me at the time the shooting took place. In reality, I had stashed it out in Baltimore County until we were ready to use it that night. I left it in an area where I knew the police wouldn't find it. My police report would be my alibi if they ever tried to question me about the shooting. It was the norm in Baltimore for someone to steal a car and use it just to commit a crime. *Damn, we some smart-ass niggas!*

After we ditched the truck somewhere in the hood in southeast D.C., we both jumped into Stink's Acura Legend and sped off on our way back to Baltimore. As we were riding and bumping Jadakiss on the radio, I pulled out a blunt and sparked it up. The blunt was a mixture of weed laced with cocaine. I took a couple of big tokes before I passed it over to Stink. He took a couple of pulls. In a few minutes, we were both lifted and talking mad shit about our future plans.

"Dog, you know these two niggas have got to be the stupidest motherfuckers in the world," I said, referring to Ty and Dayvon. "If they only knew what we had planned for their asses. They're playing right into our hands, making this so easy for us."

"Yeah, they don't even suspect we up to shit. When they finally do figure it out, both of them is gonna be deader than a motherfucker," Stink said. He took another pull off the blunt.

We had been scheming for some time to take over the DFL crew from Ty and Dayvon. In fact, it was no accident when Ty got locked up; it was Stink who called the police and tipped them off. We wanted Ty to be outta the picture because we thought it would be easier to manipulate Dayvon if Ty wasn't around. We knew how Ty got down with them guns, and we ain't want no parts of no drama with him on the streets.

With him locked up, we planned to get close to Dayvon and find a way to turn him against Ty. While they were fighting each other, we planned to wrestle control of the crew from up under their noses. We had already started buying extra weight on the side from our New York connect. We were stacking our chips in a major way to bring Ty and Dayvon a power move. We had cats on the East Side getting rid of the extra work for us.

The day Ty called us to come to see him at the jail and told us about Dayvon supposedly betraying the crew, he made me a happy man. Ty and Dayvon were already beefin'. We ain't have to do shit. Taking over now was gonna be gravy.

I guess some people might say me an' Stink had no loyalty; we wanted to be bosses without putting in the work to earn that title. Just like that old O'Jays song, we would smile in your face, all the while plotting to take your place. Maybe we were some back stabbers for real, tryin'a bring a funky move like this after all Ty and Dayvon had done for us, but whatever. It just goes to show you one thing: you can't trust nobody out in these streets.

When we got back to Baltimore later that night, Stink dropped me off at my crib then he headed out to see a li'l freak named Bootsie. His buzz from the blunt we had smoked earlier had started to wear off. That was when he called to tell me he'd made a big mistake.

When he was getting outta the car near Druid Hill Lake, he reached into his jacket pocket to get his gun. He planned to throw it in the lake. That was when he realized he must have dropped it somewhere. He was so high before he hadn't noticed his gun wasn't on him after the hit. Damn, we were fucked! I couldn't believe he did something so stupid.

We talked about it for a while, then we both said fuck it. There wasn't nothing we could do about it now. Besides, he had on gloves, so at least his prints weren't on the gun. That thought calmed us down a little. Feeling confident we were gonna still make it out all right, I hung up the phone and lit another blunt. It was time to chill after a hard night's work.

# 8
# A House Divided

I awoke to the loud buzz of my alarm clock. It was 6:00 in the morning, time to hit the block to open up shop. I knew our customers would be out there early, waiting to get them free testers to make sure our product was right. That was a guarantee, no doubt. As long as niggas were poor in the hood, they were always gonna find a way to escape reality by gettin' high. I was gonna be the cat right there to give 'em what they needed.

Before I got outta the bed, I had to do my morning ritual and roll up a flat blunt to get the day started. It's something about a nice Philly early in the morning to get me pumped up to hit the streets and get money. I'd been smoking weed since I was ten; I found it helped me to better deal with all the bullshit from these junkies and crackheads all day. They were always coming up with some lame-ass scheme, trying to get some product on the arm or for a discount, like we running a welfare office and shit. No matter how many times I told 'em no, they still kept coming back asking the same shit with a different twist. I wasn't taking no shorts; never have, never will. You can take that to the bank all day, every day.

After I jumped out of the shower, I threw on my black Azzure jeans, an oversized white T-shirt with *Pooh Dog - DFL Soldier* written on the back, and my butter Tims to get ready for work. It might not seem like work attire to a 9-to-5 cat, but in the streets, this was the perfect gear to wear.

I reached up under my pillow for my .38 and put it in my dip for protection. You gotta be ready for anything and everything. Ain't no telling when the cops might roll through or we might get hit by the stickup boys. A brotha better be prepared to stick and move at the drop of a dime, because shit is real out here. Now I was ready to hit the block to see what was poppin'.

When I stepped outta my door, all my li'l young soldiers were out, waiting and ready to go to work. Looking at them reminded me of myself a few years ago when Dayvon put me down with the game. I was young, hungry, and willing to ride to get mine, just like they were now. I could see the fire in their eyes. When you was poor and from the hood, this game might be the only way you was gonna get paid.

"Yo, Pooh. What's cracking, dog? We tryin' to get this money today. That Murder Inc. was selling like crazy last night. Them crackheads was coming back like twenty times each to get another blast of that shit," Mook said. Mook was only 14 years old, but he was big for his age. He stood almost 6 feet tall and weighed about 200 pounds. If he could only run ball, he might have had an NBA future. However, he couldn't, so he was out here trying to get rich the best way he knew how, selling crack cocaine.

Murder Inc. was what we called crack around the way. Our heroin was called Roy Jones, Jr., because it would have you knocked out on your ass so fast you wouldn't know what hit you. Every crew in the city had a unique name for whatever they were selling. We usually chose the name of some hot rap group or record label or whatever street slang was new at the time. It really didn't matter what we called it; as long as the product was right, them fiends was gonna buy it. For example, all them dope fiends gotta know was somebody overdosed off of something and they came running, wanting to know where that person got that blast from. It sounds crazy, but that's how it went out in these streets—everybody always chasing that ultimate high. They might not ever find it, but hell, they spent a lotta money along the way in pursuit of that feeling.

"I got you, li'l homey. We about to set up shop right now. Tell niggas to hold tight for a minute," I said. Just as I expected, them fiends was out there like clockwork, just waiting for things to jump off. They knew we had that good shit, and that's why they kept coming back for more.

I made my way to the stash house to get some work to hit off them young cats so they could hit the strip and get they hustle on. When I got to the stash house, I gave my man, Mo, a pound and we took care of business. After I checked the count to make sure it was right, I grabbed the package and headed out the door to hit my shorties off with the testers to get shop up and running.

"Shop up. We got them testers over here," I yelled at the top of my lungs.

The fiends was scrambling like bees flock to honey, trying to get a free blast of that rock. After I hit all the li'l homies off with their work for the day and I saw things was running right, I was straight. All I had to do was sit back and wait for them to bring me the money. Life in the hood was so sweet for a young playa in this game.

I was starting to get the munchies from the blunt I had smoked. I stepped off to hit the corner store to get some snacks. I'm a junk food addict, so I stocked up on cookies and honey buns to satisfy my sweet tooth. I walked up to the counter to pay for my stuff and to harass the Koreans just for the hell of it. I always gave them a hard time because they came into *our* hood, made money off of *us*, then always thought we came into their stores to steal from *them*. They always followed brothas around the store, thinking we were up to somethin'. Shit, if they only knew I was holding enough money to buy their little fucking corner store several times over.

When I finished paying for my snacks, I happened to look down at the newspaper and I saw the headline on the front page: *EXOTIC DANCERS SHOT DOWNTOWN.*

The headline caught my eye and I read a little further to see what had happened. It almost blew my mind when I saw the shooting happened near The Cathouse, and Jaré and Sasha were the two girls who had been shot. It said one was dead and the other was in critical condition. That shit totally blew my high. I couldn't even finish the whole article before I ran out the store and up to my girl's house.

When I got over there, Dina had already heard about the shooting on the morning news. Seeing I was pissed off, she rolled a nigga another blunt and fixed me some breakfast, trying to take my mind off this shit. She knew me well enough to know Dayvon was like a father to me. If anybody fucked with him or his peeps, then they had to deal with me.

Jaré was like a big sister to me. We had become real cool since her and Dayvon had been messing around. She used to put me down with all the chicks at the club who were easy to fuck, and she always gave me good advice whenever I had problems with a female. Sasha was cool, too, even though she had some scandalous shit with her. I knew these girls ain't have no enemies out in the streets who woulda wanted them dead. To see this shit happen to them pissed me the fuck off, and had me on a sure 'nuff revenge tip.

My street instincts were telling me this shooting had something to do with DFL business. Somebody was trying to send us a message. Everybody knew Jaré messed with Dayvon, and no nigga dared to step to her tryin'a holla, because Day wasn't having that shit. That's why I knew this was a personal thing. My gut feeling was one of them jealous-ass East Side crews was tryin'a bring us some drama because they saw us getting all this money over here. I was gonna put the word out on the street to see what I could find out before I called Dayvon. The block was about to be hot for real if those niggas wanted war with us.

I tried calling Stink and Li'l Jay to see if they had heard anything about what had happened, but neither one of them fools answered their cell phones. Them niggas be on some other shit most of the time, so I didn't think nothing of it. They were always together, doing God knows what. I wasn't that tight with them because I liked to ride solo, but we always had each other's backs when it counted. If one of us had beef, then we all had beef. That's how Day and Ty always taught us to roll. Fuck it. I would catch up with them later. For right now, I had to get my mind right to figure out what my next move was gonna be. It was time to spark another L.

It didn't take long for word to get around on the streets of Baltimore about a murder, or about who got beef with who. Still, I wasn't prepared for the 411 when it got back to me as to what actually went down with the shooting. After I checked out my sources and made sure the info was legit, I had to sit back and wonder how some shit like this could happen with my crew, right in front of me, and I ain't know nothing about it. I had to hear about this shit secondhand. It took me a few hours, but then all the pieces fell into place.

I got the word from my man, Brian, another young hustler from South B'more who I was cool with, about who had planned the shooting and who actually put in the work. He told me he got the info from one of his homies, Joel, who was locked up with Ty. He told me about the argument that took place between Ty and Dayvon in the visiting room out at the jail.

At first I was kinda mad at Dayvon for leaving town and not telling me about what went on between him and Ty. I thought we were tighter than that. Then I had to realize he was a smart dude; if he didn't tell me shit, then he must have had his reasons. I was a soldier in every sense, so I had to respect his place as the boss of this crew and not question his judgment.

Brian also told me how Ty was spreading the word in the joint that Dayvon was a snitch and not to be trusted. Ty put Li'l Jay and Stink up to shooting Jaré to send a message to Dayvon, and Dayvon's sister was next.

I couldn't believe what I was hearing. I knew Dayvon better than any of them other cats, except maybe Ty, because I was around him a lot. I knew he wasn't no snitch. He had always been a standup cat who kept it true to the game, no matter what. I knew somebody must have put some crazy shit in Ty's head to make him snap like that. Either that or he had something up his sleeve Dayvon didn't know about. As ruthless as Ty was, it wouldn't surprise me if he wanted to knock Dayvon off to have all the money we were making to himself. As long as I was alive, though, things wasn't gonna go down like that.

When Brian told me about Li'l Jay and Stink and how they were going around telling cats they were gonna be the new bosses of the DFL crew in a minute, the picture started to become clear. Something else was going on that maybe Dayvon or Ty didn't even know about. I always had a feeling them niggas was some grimy motherfuckers on the low, but I'd let it slide because they never got outta pocket with me.

I could tell they were jealous because me and Dayvon were tight and he made me a lieutenant just like them, even though I was like five or six years younger than them. Shit, it wasn't my fault Ty and Dayvon appreciated the work I put in for the family. Game recognize game, and now their hating asses was gonna pay for what they did to my homegirls.

Knowing what I had learned, I was glad when I called Kiera to find out she was out of town for her summer break, visiting one of her girlfriends in Florida. I told her Dayvon wanted her to stay down there for another week or so to have some fun. I wired her some money and said it was from him. I never let on exactly why she should stay, but she didn't care anyway. She was used to him spoiling her. Plus, she was having mad fun out on the beach.

With that taken care of, I had to contact Dayvon and let him know what was going on. I tried to reach him on his cell, but the phone just rang. I didn't leave a message, because I knew how the Feds could tap a cell and retrieve messages when they wanted to build a case against someone. Knowing Dayvon, he was probably off with some broad, gettin' laid. I would hit him up later, to give him a heads up and find out what he wanted me to do. He was the one who brought me into this game, and I would ride with him 'til I die out this motherfucker.

# 9
# Too Good To Be True

The last week or so had been totally off the chain, hanging out with Cheri in the ATL. I hadn't had this much fun in a minute. I was getting a chance to get some sophisticated pussy and, at the same time, ease some of the stress that had been on my mind, dealing with this street drama. Cheri had taken me to every top-notch restaurant in town as well as shown me all of the hot spots to cop some new gear to take back with me to B'more. She knew I liked to hear poetry and spoken word, so she took me to the Apache Café in downtown Atlanta to hear some of the hottest poets on the East Coast. This girl definitely had class and knew how to treat a playa of my stature. I would have to keep her around for a minute.

Hanging out with Cheri, I also got a chance to develop a cultured side I didn't show to my boys. They just wouldn't understand. If they knew I liked to go to art showcases or plays, they'd think I was soft. I couldn't afford for that to happen in my line of work; ain't no way for a man to show an interest in art and be a thug at the same time. I almost had to live a double life just to have some fun.   That was why I was getting outta this game; so I could just do me and not have to worry about these unsophisticated fools.

When I was growing up, my parents used to take me, my brother, and my sister to the zoo, museum, or amusement parks all the time. Most inner city kids aren't exposed to the different cultural things I had been privileged to see in my life. I didn't appreciate it back then, but over time I had acquired a liking for art shows and all of the Black plays, like the ones by Tyler Perry. I was starting to understand the things my parents told me about being blessed to have the finer things in life and not taking them for granted. Back then, I wasn't trying to hear it because I felt like I was a square if I showed an interest in things like painting and poetry. I guess I was trying to fit in and was willing to deny my stable home life to be down with Ty and our crew.

They say hindsight is 20/20, and now I was starting to regret the foolish choices that had led me down the road I'd taken. I was hoping it wasn't too late for me to get back on track and redirect my life.

I looked over at my watch and it read 11:00 in the morning. It was Monday and Cheri had already left for work. One of her coworkers came to pick her up and she left me the keys to her BMW so I could use her whip while she was out gettin' that money. I was wondering what in the hell I could get into, seeing as though I had another three days before I planned on returning home to Baltimore. I was beginning to think I could get used to this, being free and clear to think about life outside of all the street drama. I didn't have to worry about who wanted what from me or whether or not the police were following my every move. Down here, I could just chill and enjoy living life on my own terms. However, I knew all of this was just temporary and I would have some madness to deal with when I got back to the real world in B'more.

I reached over the side of the bed to retrieve my cell phone off the floor. That was when I realized Pooh had called me twice. He must have called the night before when I was gettin' my freak on with Cheri, because I hadn't heard the phone ring. That girl made so much damn noise, screaming and yelling when I was giving her the pipe, it was hard to hear anything over her loud ass.

I knew something had to be up, because Pooh was a reliable soldier who could handle business while I was gone. He wouldn't disturb me when I was on vacation unless it was something he felt he couldn't handle alone. With that in mind, I picked up my cell and dialed his number to get the 411. He answered on the second ring.

"What's up, li'l homey? How are things in B'more?"

"Yo, you need to get back here like on the double, 'cause shit is thick out here. Jaré got shot. Her and Sasha. This shit is crazy. I can't explain it on this phone, but you need to get here now, nigga!"

"I'm on the first thing smoking outta here. I'ma call you as soon as I get back in town. Hold down the fort until I get there."

I was in a state of shock when he told me Jaré had been shot, but I also knew Pooh couldn't give me too much information over the phone. He knew our rules about that: Never say too much over the phone, because that's a quick way to get indicted. As I put the phone down, I tried to do all I could not to burst into tears. That fight lasted all of a minute before teardrops rained down my cheeks. I went into the bathroom to get a tissue to wipe my face and blow my nose. I had to regain my composure.

All types of ill thoughts were running through my head. I was wondering if Jaré was dead and who could possibly wanna do something like this to her. I was also concerned about Sasha, because we were mad cool. Whoever did this was gonna pay. I was hoping the shooting didn't have anything to do with me and my lifestyle.

It was at that moment I started to realize just how much I cared about Jaré. Just hearing about something bad happening to her made my heart sink deep down in my chest. Thoughts of Cheri and all the fun we'd had in the past week faded from my mind, even though I was still in her crib and about to drive her car. Could this be love, or was I just trippin'? I tried to tell myself a playa of my status don't fall in love, but I was hardly convinced.

I jumped up off the bed and got into the shower to get ready to catch a flight home. As I was getting dressed, I started thinking of a lie I could tell Cheri about why I was leaving all of a sudden. I knew she was gonna get all hyped up and shit and start crying. She knew I had a weakness for women when they cry. She threw a fit every time I left her, but this time it wouldn't matter. I had more pressing business to tend to back home. Her ass would just have to get over it with a quickness.

I had a hard time getting free from Cheri when I went to take her the car keys and tell her I was leaving earlier than I had planned. She did just as I expected, putting on a dramatic performance that would have made Halle Berry proud. She was going on and on about how much she was starting to care about me and how much she wanted me to move to Atlanta so we could have a real relationship. I just nodded my head as though I was listening to her rambling. The whole time, my mind was elsewhere, thinking about Jaré. Cheri's sideshow went on for about thirty minutes before I broke free and told her I had to bounce and handle business back home. Damn, the life of a playa was so hard sometimes.

After I got outta the game, I might have to give this up too.

It was about 5:00 in the evening when my flight arrived at BWI airport outside of Baltimore. I waited about 45 minutes for Pooh to arrive and put me down with what was going on. My ears were burning and my mind was in a daze when he told me what Ty had done. My body felt totally numb for a few as Pooh ran down the 411 on what actually went down with the whole situation. I knew Ty could be ruthless, but I never thought he would take things to this level with me.

After Pooh told me Jaré was pregnant by me and my baby died because of the trauma from her injuries, all I had was hate on my mind. I was ready to kill Ty and anyone else who got in my way. Anybody could get it if they said the wrong thing to me. I wasn't gonna spare a soul.

I remembered before I left, Jaré had been trying to tell me something. Now I knew what it was. She was trying to tell me I was going to be a father. I wished I had taken the time to listen to her then, because maybe none of this would've went down. Maybe I wouldn't have left town and I would have been there to protect her from this shit.

Jaré was always good to a nigga and never asked for much in return. She put up with all of my shit with me not wanting to commit to her. All she wanted to give me was the beautiful gift of a child. There were no words I could think of with all my smooth talk that would make up for the pain I had brought into her life. *Charge it all to da game,* was all I could say, because I had no answers.

All types of memories were going through my head. I thought about all the wild shit me and Ty had done together throughout the years. I thought about all the parties, getting high, and bitches we had shared. Growing up in this game together we had been inseparable, but now, because of his stupid-ass paranoid delusions, we were about to become the worst enemies.

How the fuck could he fix his lips to say I was a snitch? Maybe the fact that I was trying to leave the game had him feeling insecure about running the crew all by himself. Still, he knew how I was, and I was as loyal to my homies as loyal could get. Blood in and blood out was how I had rolled with him ever since we got into the game. While he'd been locked up, I made sure Gena and his son were taken care of and got everything they needed and wanted. In return, he wound up stabbing me in the back like this. This nigga had to pay for this shit he done set in motion. He hit my shorty and he planned to come and get me? I don't think so!

I always had a suspicion Ty thought I had a weak side to me, since I wasn't your typical street hustler born in the hood. I'm not saying he didn't have love for me, but he felt like he had to do the dirty work whenever it needed to be done, because he thought I wasn't built for it. It wasn't that I was afraid of the war side of this game; it was just that I was more of a thinker and I tried to avoid beef whenever possible. Ty, on the other hand, lived for the drama of all the shootouts and beefs we had with the competition. It was like he got high off that shit, the same way a junkie feels when he goes into a dope nod. Ty used to joke that I was a lover and he was a fighter, but he was about to find out how wrong he was. I was a nice guy and all, but don't get it twisted; I would get down for mine when I needed to.

Before I dealt with Ty and his bitch ass, Li'l Jay and Stink were the first ones on my list of motherfuckers to be erased. Just think, before we let them get down with us, they were getting pimped by Ice over on the East Side. Ice had them cats over there working for $100 a day. They wasn't pushing no fly-ass whips, flossin' no jewels, gettin' bitches, or none of that shit. When they came to us crying broke, we put them on. That was when they started seeing some real money. Bitches was trying to holla just on the strength of the fact that they were down with DFL. They started pushing the Lexuses and Acuras, and niggas was respecting their gangsta because of our reputation. Now these turncoat motherfuckers had the nerve to think they were gonna flip the script and take this shit from me and

Ty after we taught them the game? They had it comin' to 'em raw with no Vaseline.

My mind was all fucked up now, and I had to put my plans to get outta the game on hold. I had to hold court to let motherfuckers know I wasn't going out like no sucker-ass nigga. This situation just taught me a lesson about this game that was as real as life gets. No matter what good intentions you might have once you get into this game, the madness of this life doesn't leave room to make an exit without negative consequences. I got into this game to get paid and to get out of it with no scars. Now I saw you gotta pay to play, and sometimes the price might be your own life, or the lives of your loved ones.

I had Pooh drop me off at one of my many apartments only he knew about. In the drug game, it's never good to let too many niggas know where you lay your head at all the time. That's a good way to get caught slippin'. I had him take me out to P.G. County to the condo I kept when I wanted to get away from the city. I had to lay low for a few to get my thoughts together and plot my course of action. I told him not to say nothing to nobody about me being back in town. I planned to maneuver under the cloak of darkness when I got my revenge on all these fools. I gave him a pound and sent him back to the city with his orders. I knew he would follow them to the letter, because Pooh was a soldier like that.

*Jaré! Jaré! Jaré! Damn, girl, why you had to get caught up in my shit?   Because of me, my child is dead.  I wish you knew how much I loved you. I wish I could do it all over again.* My conscience was fucking with me in a major way. Inside my condo and feeling stressed out, I lit up a blunt and just smoked all night as the misery set in.

# 10
# Drama in P.G. County

I'd been out in P.G. County for about three weeks, getting my strategy together to deal with this situation. All my orders to the crew were still coming through Pooh.  Nobody else, besides my family, knew I was back in Maryland.

I'd had a long talk with my father earlier in the week.  We attempted to mend some fences between us.  He offered his regards with respect to Jaré. We talked for a long time about how we both missed the close relationship we used to have when I was a little kid, and how we wished we could have that again. My mother felt pretty much the same way. Even though she was angry with me for the choices I had made in my life, I knew deep down inside she could never totally give up on me. A good mother would always keep a glimmer of hope alive for her child, no matter how many bad things he might have done. Her and my pops just wanted me to get my life together and do the right thing. I told them about my plans to get outta the game. I also told them before I could do that, I had some unfinished business to tend to. They both just said a prayer for me and hoped I was careful in whatever I chose to do.

The first thing I had to do was be honest with myself about my feelings for Jaré. I couldn't afford for my thoughts to be sidetracked by my love for her. I had to be on top of my game, because things were about to get hectic. The easiest way to get knocked off of ya grind out in these streets was not to be thinking clearly. That's when a playa could miss out on things that might make the difference between catching a case or being carried out in a closed casket.

I reached inside my dresser drawer and pulled out the letter Jaré had sent to me before she left town. I was still not clear about how she had been able to leave the hospital against the doctor's wishes and without the police knowing her whereabouts. They obviously wanted to question her about the shooting. I tried to see her at the hospital, but her family wouldn't let me into her room. Apparently, she told them she didn't want to see me or have anything to do with me. I had to respect her wishes.

I sat and read her letter for the umpteenth time as my pain soaked in and memories of her cluttered my thoughts. Her words came down on me like a ton of bricks. I felt every blow she sent my way. I was trying to make some sense outta this whole situation, wondering how it got this far outta hand. I had to come up with a way to fix it.

Dear Dayvon,

My aunt and my mother told me you tried to come and see me at the hospital. I thought it was best that we not see each other, because at this time in my life, I really have no words for you. I really can't explain how much pain being involved with you has caused me in the last few weeks. First, I lost my—excuse me, our baby—and then I lost my best friend.

I asked God what the hell I did to deserve this type of misery. I just couldn't come up with an answer. All I knew was I was another young, dumb female who fell in love with a hustler and got herself caught up in his bullshit lifestyle.

All I ever wanted to do was love you, but you never wanted to give me the commitment I really needed and deserved. You knew how I felt about you, even though we said we were not exclusive in our relationship. I knew you had other females in your life, but I still stuck in there, hoping you would get tired of running around in the streets and settle down with me. Never once in the whole time we were seeing each other did you hear about me fucking around with somebody else. I had big plans for us, and look what they wound up costing me. I might not ever use my right arm the same again, and I have a bullet permanently lodged in my spine that causes me so much pain.

*Since Sasha ain't around, I have no reason to stay in Baltimore. In spite of whatever pain I'm feeling inside, I have to be strong for my son because he needs me right now.*

*You don't have to worry about me telling the police shit, even though I saw who did this to me. I know you'll figure it out and handle your business accordingly.*

*I never doubted you cared about me (maybe even loved me in your own way), but I'm asking that you please not try to contact me. I just can't deal with the sight of your face right now. I hope I've made myself clear and you understand where I'm coming from.*

*I'm moving on with my life and leaving you in my past. This is the way it has to be. In other words, what I'm trying to say is FUCK OFF!*

*Jaré*

There was nothing I could say to deny what was in her letter. It was all true; I was guilty of everything she said about me. I never gave her the love and respect she called for. I was too busy being a playa and doing my thing. She had every right to not wanna see me anymore, but I knew this letter was just her way of venting her anger. Once she calmed down, she would realize she couldn't fight her love for me. Over time, she would forgive me. I was just gonna give her space to get some stability in her life and then I would get her back. In the meantime, I could square away this situation with Ty.

I made a trip upstate to New York to cop a couple of bricks of raw coke because everybody's supply was running low. Our main supplier, Hector, always hit us off with some quality product. His prices were right on time. Hector was a short Dominican dude who kinda reminded me of Al Pacino when he played Tony Montana in the movie *Scarface*. Hector had a "take no shit" type of attitude, but he was always fair with us. I guess he liked the fact that we always had his money on time for him and we came back on a regular basis to buy more product.

After I went up north to hit Hector off with the loot, I sent Pooh and a mule to pick up the coke and bring it back to Baltimore. I wasn't gonna be as stupid as Ty and let the knockers catch me dirty. I was too smart for that. Ever since I was a shorty and I stopped working them corners, you wouldn't ever find me handling no product myself. Besides, that was what we paid our workers for. It was one of the benefits of being the boss. These young cats knew the risks involved in this game, and they were aware of the consequences if they got caught. They knew that along with the money and fame came the chance they might catch a bid. That's just how life goes.

Pooh went to hit up Li'l Jay and Stink with some more product, and noticed they both seemed kinda nervous. He said they damn near shitted on themselves when he asked them if they had heard about the shooting. They pretended they didn't know about it, but he knew they were frontin'. I had showed Pooh how to play a nigga outta position so well he wouldn't even know he had been played. From the way they acted and their body language, Pooh knew they were guilty. However, he never said a word about his suspicions. He just remained cool, calm, and collected.

He did tell them I had put a hit out on the shooters and whoever planned it. When they heard that news, he said he could smell the fear as it seeped through their pores. They asked Pooh where I was. He just told them I was outta town on family business, but I had come back just long enough to make sure shop was up and running for everybody.

I made sure Pooh put 24-hour security on Kiera so no harm would come to my baby sis. He got Big Lou and Hank to follow her everywhere she went. She would never know she had a shadow following her, because they were just that good at what they did.

Big Lou stood about 6 feet 4 inches tall and weighed around 250 pounds. He was an ex-boxer over at Mack Lewis' gym. He could lay a nigga out cold with one shot to the dome. He perfected what we called the one-hitta quitta.

On the other hand, Hank was only about 5 feet 6 inches tall and weighed around 140 pounds. His father was a Vietnam veteran who taught him how to shoot a gun from the time he was nine years old. Raised in North Carolina, Hank was an ex-Green Beret, dishonorably discharged from the service. When we wanted somebody tailed or killed discreetly, he was the man to call. With these two cats watching my baby girl, I knew she would be safe.

The one thing I don't think Ty realized when he started this war was I had one big advantage over him. You see, Pooh's crew in the Village had over a hundred soldiers alone. I knew Pooh would ride with me no matter what. I also knew I had the loyalty of all of his shorties with me, if they ever had to choose sides between Ty or me. Pooh had a string of young killas around him who were quick to body a motherfucker once Pooh gave the order. They were all down to do whatever for a come-up in this game. One thing about these young cats in Baltimore was they wouldn't hesitate to pull out that heat and squeeze on a nigga, just for G.P. You stared at one of them wrong and you were liable to get your cap peeled. That was probably why the murder rate was so high in Baltimore.

Pooh's crew was the biggest crew we had, and they made the most money out of all of our workers.

Li'l Jay and stink had about thirty or forty cats apiece in their cliques up on Park Heights and Liberty Heights, but they were no match for Pooh's team. Ronnie-O's crew was the smallest. He only had about twenty soldiers on his team, but don't get that twisted. They held their own down on Pennsylvania and Gold Street. I knew I could count on Ronnie-O's loyalty, because him and Pooh were tight. With about sixty percent of our most thorough soldiers with me, and the fact that Ty wasn't out here on the streets himself, he didn't stand a chance to knock me outta the game as easily as he had planned.

Ty probably chose Li'l Jay and Stink to carry out his orders because they were two stupid-ass flunkies he controlled outta fear. He was the one who had suggested we put them down with us when they were working out on the East Side. Ty had a thing about always trying to punk a nigga into doing something just to satisfy his own ego and make himself feel like a man. On the other hand, I treated all of our soldiers like men and gave them proper respect. One thing I knew about these young cats today was fear didn't last long with them before they started plotting on your ass and came for your spot on the throne. Li'l Jay and Stink were living proof of that, right in front of his eyes. His rage and his pride just didn't allow him to see it.

While I was busy plotting my revenge, I called Nikki to come over and keep me company. She was fine as hell; one of them island girls with a dark-skinned, even-toned complexion from being out in the tropical sun all day, growing up in Jamaica. She was a hairstylist, and her specialty was doing braids and extensions. She owned a beauty salon with her sister in P.G. County and they did pretty well for themselves. All of my women had it going on professionally in one way or another. One thing I couldn't stand was a broke-ass bitch who always had her hand out, asking for something. I didn't mind spending money on a woman, but it had to be because I wanted to and not because she needed me to do it.

Nikki's body stopped traffic everywhere she went. Watching her walk would have you bobbing your head up and down, trying to follow the rhythm of her big breasts. They bounced around like two big bowling balls, but they were perfectly shaped in a way only God could have done. It was something about them Caribbean women and their sexy accents that just did something to me. Add that to the way they danced all sensual up in those dancehall clubs; they just put me in a state of mind to fuck. That winding move they did with their hips was a killa. Nikki would get me every time with that when she was on top of me, riding my dick. She just took the sex to another level for me.

"Yo, Nikki, why don't you cook me some of that curry chicken wit' peas and rice, ma?" I asked.

"Cook it yourself, motherfucker. Or ask that bitch Jaré to cook it for you. Me not cook you nuthin', you bastard, you," she responded. Her Jamaican accent was in full effect. That meant she was angry with a brotha.

"Come on, boo. You know I ain't mean what I said. It was an accident." I was trying to make up for my major fuck-up the night before.

The night had started off fine. When she came over, she was wearing a short mini-skirt and a T-shirt with no bra. Her nipples were poking through her shirt like they were trying to escape. They had *bite me* all over them. Her ass was doing a soul clap of its own as she walked about the house. We smoked a few spliffs before I took her out on the balcony for an erotic treat. She loved for me to sit her on the rail and spread her thick, athletic legs across my shoulders while I ate her pussy, enjoying the midnight air. She screamed so loud I knew my neighbors must have heard.

"Damn, Dayvon. Eat this pussy, rude boy. You know me love you long time."

I gave her what she came to get when I unzipped my shorts and inserted all of me inside her pleasure palace. I lifted her off the rail and carried her over to the lounge chair. My dick never came out of her pussy the whole time as I continued to tear her insides up with force, just the way she liked it. She loved every stroke. She let me know by digging her nails into my back. I turned her over on the lounge chair and she grabbed onto the rail. I wanted to hit that ass from behind. She put her legs up in the air and balanced her feet up against the sliding door. I was getting turned on watching that phat ass jiggle with my every stroke. *Damn, this some good-ass pussy!* I was getting more intoxicated by the wetness of her walls. Cum started to flow down her leg like a river.

"Damn, Jaré. I'm about to come, baby. All this love juice is for you," I said. I released a tidal wave of semen all over her big, chocolate ass.

"What the fuck did you just say? Who the fuck did you just call me?" Nikki asked. She turned around and pushed me away with all of her might.

"Nothing, Jaré—I mean Nikki." I was digging a deeper hole for myself when I called her out of her name a second time.

She got up from the chair and ran into the house, heading for the bathroom. Tears were welling up in her eyes and her rage was building. You ain't seen rage until you seen a Jamaican woman upset. She cursed me out with so much venom and called me so many names I didn't know what to say. She went into the kitchen and started throwing anything she could pick up. Pots, pans, and silverware all came flying at me. After she was finished, she stormed out the front door.

Nikki said she was through with me, but I knew better. I had her sprung on the dick. I knew once she calmed down she would be back for another dose of this good lovin'. It took a little smooth talk on my part to get her to come back and see me the next night, but sometimes you gotta do what you gotta do. All that attitude and anger she had inside just set the stage for some good make-up fucking later on. And this time I would be careful to call this Jamaican sistah by the right name.

# 11
# When Shit Hits the Fan

Ty was all messed up in the head. His mind was in a state of panic as he took another hit off his jailhouse cigarette, rolled up in Tops paper. He had just come back from seven days in solitary confinement for fighting with another inmate named Chauncey. He bumped into Ty by mistake in the chow line, but he didn't apologize. Ty took that as disrespect and gave Chauncey the ass whippin' of a lifetime. Poor Chauncey had to have forty-five stitches after Ty cracked him over the head with a lock in a sock. Chauncey suffered several broken ribs and his eye was permanently damaged once Ty was done with him.

Chauncey never stood a chance against Ty. He was a small dude, only about 5 feet 6 inches tall and weighing less than 150 pounds. However, what Ty didn't know was Chauncey was connected with some major players up in Philly. His family was heavy in the drug game up there. They were quick to exact pain on anybody who fucked with one of theirs. They were called the South Side Killas and known for doing just that, catching bodies on a regular. One day, Ty would regret fucking with Chauncey.

Most of the time, Ty got away with his bullying and quick-tempered rampages because a lotta cats in the joint feared him. Since he'd been locked down, Ty had managed to put together a nice-sized clique that controlled all of the drug trade at the jail. Just as he did on the streets, Ty knew how to stack his paper in a major way.

Any fool who told you that you can't get drugs in jail was lying. In every jail in this country, there were C.O.'s who were willing to risk their jobs for some extra loot by bringing it in themselves, or looking the other way when deals went down. Either that or a prisoner could find some dope fiend broad who was willing to stuff drugs in her pussy or asshole to bring it to him just to get a free high. In other words, where there was a will, there was always a way to make it happen. The game don't change in the joint; you just gotta adjust the way you play it.

Ty paid a couple of crooked C.O.'s who smuggled drugs into the jail for him. This operation was totally separate from the DFL crew. He never mentioned it to Dayvon and didn't plan to. This was his own thing, and he didn't see a need to share the profits.

Ty was pissed at himself because his plans for Dayvon didn't go as he had expected them to. He read about the shooting in the paper after it went down and he knew this thing could get ugly. The fact that Jaré survived the shooting made him nervous. If by chance she saw anything the night of the shooting and told the police, there was a chance the trail could lead back to him. Even worse, if she told Dayvon what she saw, Ty knew that spelled disaster for him. Dayvon easily had an advantage over him, since Ty was locked up. Dayvon could maneuver around more and make a lot more things happen. Ty now had to think about Gena and his son's safety.

Ty was up early one particular morning because he couldn't sleep at all the night before. He was busy thinking about what his next move was gonna be. He had to make some sense outta this mess Li'l Jay and Stink had created. *If those motherfuckers had just followed my plans to the letter then things wouldn't be so messy right now. All they had to do was kill Jaré and then take care of Kiera the next day, right after I gave them their orders. Everything would've been smooth sailing,* Ty thought. Instead of doing as they were told, they procrastinated and waited around a few days before doing anything.

By that time, Kiera had left town to go to Miami. Ty learned this from Gena. Gena and Kiera were friends who hung out on occasion. In fact, Gena was supposed to go to Miami with Kiera, but changed her plans at the last minute because she couldn't find a babysitter. With Kiera outta reach, Li'l Jay and Stink would have to wait until she returned to Baltimore.

However, that wasn't their worst mistake. To make matters worse, they had wound up killing the wrong person. When they did bring Jaré a move, they weren't expecting Sasha. But when they saw her, they were supposed to make sure both of them were dead before they left the scene. Leaving witnesses behind was an easy way to get the electric chair.

Ty got the word from one of his police contacts that the cops had found one of them fools' guns up the street from the murder scene. They were waiting on a fingerprint match to come back from the crime lab. *How the fuck could they be so stupid and leave a gun near a murder scene?* Ty asked himself.

He cursed himself for trusting these two idiots. As it turned out, the police didn't find any prints on the gun, but they found a few on the bullets that weren't fired from the gun, as well as on the shell casings found around the car. When the prints came back and were identified, there was no telling how they would react or what they might do. One of them, if not both of them, would definitely drop a dime to avoid the weight of a murder charge. They were gonna have to be dealt with. Ty had them coming to see him that day to try to size up what they were thinking.

As Ty made his way down to the visiting room, he wondered whether or not he had jumped the gun by trying to bring Dayvon such a funky move. Memories of all of the things they had done together throughout the years were flowing through his head and fucking up his ability to think clearly. In all of the time he'd known Dayvon, there was never one time Dayvon didn't have his back when it was needed. Ty could depend on him for just about anything.

When Dayvon came to see him, talking all that talk about wanting to get outta the game, Ty's mind just snapped. As far as Ty was concerned, the only cats who got out of the game were older dudes like his uncle or a snitch. Since he knew Dayvon wasn't an O.G., he figured he had to be a snitch. In the drug game, a brotha's mind could play tricks like that, especially when he was locked up. He could mistake friends for enemies and enemies for friends. It was just the nature of the beast.

No matter how he looked at it, Ty knew what was done was done, and it was too late to turn back. The wheels of fate were already turning and this thing had to end one way or another. Of course, Ty planned to come out on top.

"Visitor for Tyrone Adams," Officer Presbulewski said over the intercom.

Officer Presbulewski was a straight racist, redneck C.O. who hated Blacks with a passion. He made it his personal business to fuck with Ty whenever he could. He was tall, lanky, and looked somewhat like Jim Carey. He had freckles all over his face and red hair. He'd been a C.O. for fifteen years and loved his job. He got a thrill outta whippin' on the black inmates just for the hell of it. The word *nigga* was a regular part of his vocabulary.

Ty made his way through the steel door to the visiting room and handed the C.O. his pass.

"Hey, Adams, you got two monkeys waiting for you. They look like they need to be fed," Presbulewski said with a smirk.

"Where? I don't see your mother and father over there," Ty shot back. Ty didn't give a fuck what kinda power Presbulewski had in the jail. He didn't take no shit from none of them C.O.'s. He was willing to take an ass whipping from a gang of them to make it clear he was just as much of a man as they were.

"Watch it, Adams. You might wind up going to sleep tonight and not waking up."

"Bring it, motherfucker. You want some, come get some, and you gonna sure 'nuff take some."

Ty made his way through the visiting room and over to the table where Dumb and Dumber (his nicknames for Li'l Jay and Stink) were seated. Li'l Jay was a stocky and compact fella. He was built kinda like Mike Tyson. Stink was around the same height, but about 20 pounds lighter and with a lot less muscle. The only thing that stood out about him was his reddish complexion and his buck-toothed, goofy smile. They both looked scared as hell when Ty walked into the room. They sat in silence as he pulled up a chair and took a seat. A feeling of darkness now covered the room.

"So, what the fuck happened?" Ty asked them.

"Yo, we thought them girls was dead, dog. All of them shots we let off, we were sure we got 'em," Li'l Jay replied.

"You *thought* they were dead? You were supposed to *know* they were dead before you rolled out. You was supposed to hit Jaré, not Sasha. Y'all done fucked up major," Ty said. He felt like bitch-smacking both of their asses, but he didn't wanna catch another ticket. He was trying to make parole in a few months.

"What you worried about, yo? Jaré done left town and she ain't say shit to the cops. She can't anyhow, because she ain't see shit. You need to be worried about Dayvon. He done put a hit out on whoever did the shooting."

"I'll deal with that later. Which one of y'all jackasses dropped your gun on the scene? Once they run the prints they found, who you think they gonna pin this on? Y'all gotta eat this charge," Ty said.

Stink sat back in his chair in a state of shock. He wondered how Ty found out about him losing his gun. He hadn't told anyone but Li'l Jay. The blood rushed to Stink's forehead. He was worried his mishap might wind up sitting him down for a long stretch. Nonetheless, he sat back in his chair and tried to hide his fear as he responded to Ty.

"I ain't even worried about that gun demonstration. If it's prints on that gun, they damn sure ain't mine. I had on gloves."

"Yeah, but they got your prints on the bullets, dumb ass. You still fucked. How the fuck you gonna go to take somebody out and not empty your whole chamber into 'em?" Ty asked.

"Fuck you, nigga. We ain't taking this charge alone. We only agreed to do this because you said we were gonna be running the show with you once Dayvon was outta the picture. I ain't copping out to shit!" Stink insisted.

"Nigga, who the fuck do you think you raising up on?" Ty asked.

"Man, kill that noise. We was doing you a favor," Li'l Jay interjected. He wanted Stink to know he had his back.

"Y'all better keep my name off of ya lips or else y'all some dead motherfuckers. I put that shit on my son. Who the fuck done told either one of y'all that you got the balls to talk shit to me?" Ty asked. He saw they no longer feared him, but he was still trying to hold his ground.

"Whatever, man. We tired of you talking to us like shit. We ain't the same li'l niggas you knew three years ago. We got our own plans. Your time on top done came and went. You need to be worried about Dayvon and not dropping the soap," Li'l Jay said. He was talking mad trash.

"Fool, you work for me. I made you and I can break you in the streets. Let me find out you bitches is tryin'a cross a nigga!"

"Consider yourself crossed, fool. Crossed the fuck outta the game," Stink said.

Ty got up from the table and took a swing at Stink. He just missed connecting with his jaw as Stink swerved outta the way. The guards rushed over to restrain Ty and to take him back to his cell. Li'l Jay and Stink walked out of the visiting room, knowing there was no turning back at this point. They wanted a war, and that was exactly what they got. Only problem was they didn't know who was their worst enemy, Dayvon or Ty. Young and dumb, they really didn't give damn. All they knew was they wanted to be on top and were willing to do whatever was necessary to get there.

Back in his cell, Ty was ready to hurt something. He never expected for this thing to turn out like it had. He thought his reputation on the streets would make them niggas think twice about crossing him, but here they were, talking cash shit right to his face. "Them niggas is dead," was all he kept saying to himself. He walked out of his cell to the payphone to make a call. The phone rang five times before Gena picked it up.

"Hello."

The recorded operator's voice chimed in to let Gena know it was Ty calling collect from the jail. She reluctantly accepted the charges.

"Damn, bitch. Why the fuck did it take you so long to answer the damn phone? Where the hell have you been for the past week? I've been calling you every night," Ty grumbled.

"First of all, nigga, don't be calling here this late at night with no bullshit. Second of all, wherever I've been at ain't none of your damn business," she answered.

Ty wanted to leap through the phone and grab Gena by her neck for coming outta her mouth like that. In the five years he had been messing with her, he had whipped her ass more than enough times whenever she ran her mouth too much. Gena gave as much as she got, though. She was a big girl and could hold her own whenever their arguments came to blows. That was part of the reason why Ty liked her so much—this girl could scrap. He wanted a ride or die chick around who would be ready to throw hands if he needed her to have his back.

Gena had grown up rough on the streets of Baltimore. She had five brothers; she was the only girl. Their father was locked down in Cumberland, Maryland, serving a 30-year sentence for bank robbery. He had been locked up since she was 5 years old. It was after his incarceration that her mother started drinking and shooting heroin.

Her mother was a drug addict and an alcoholic who beat on Gena and verbally abused her all the time. She was trying to destroy Gena's self-esteem, the same way her drug use had done to her. Every time she looked in her daughter's face, Gena's beauty reminded her of her own missed opportunities, so she took her failures out on Gena. She died when Gena was 9 years old.

With no parents around to raise them, Gena and her brothers were forced to do whatever was necessary to survive. That included selling drugs, boosting, armed robbery, and stealing cars. If it was a caper to be pulled, then they were down for it. They had to if they wanted to keep a roof over their heads.

It was this drama in her life that attracted her to Ty. He could relate to her pain and she could relate to his. The problem was neither one of them ever learned how to truly love another person. They only knew how to express that crazy, drama-filled type of affection. Gena had sworn that she would try to make a better life for herself and her son, so he wouldn't have to struggle and grow up without love the way she had. She was headed in the wrong direction with Ty.

Ty and Gena had one of those love/hate relationships. They both fed off of each other's craziness. It was normal to see them having a knock down, drag 'em out fight in the streets. He cheated on her with other females and she cheated on him with other males. However, sooner than anyone could bat an eye, the two of them would be back together, as though nothing had happened. They were the Bobby and Whitney of the hood. They both lived fast and loved hard—a couple made in hell.

"Girl, don't act like you don't know who the fuck I am and you forgot what I can do to you, even though I'm locked up. I still pay the bills up in there. Remember that," Ty reminded her.

"Nigga, you ain't gonna do shit. I do what I want, when I want, and with whom I want. I'm a grown-ass woman," Gena shot back. She was trying to get a rise outta Ty. It was working.

"Yeah, a'ight. Let me find out that you got another nigga up in there around my son. Be stupid if you want."

"Let me tell me you something, and I hope you never forget it. This pussy belongs to me, and if I decide to give it to somebody else, it ain't none of your damn business. Just 'cause you locked up don't mean that I am. As a matter of fact, you're interrupting my flow right now. Daddy, come over here and tell him what you about to do this pussy," she said. She motioned for her male companion to take the phone. Gena liked to play with fire. This time, she was gonna get burned.

"Hello. Yeah, nigga, what you want? I'm about to tear this pussy up. Take your ass back up in that cell with your bunk buddy and let him blow you," the man on the other end of the phone said to Ty.

"What the fuck! Dayvon, that better not be your ass up in there bonin' my girl! You a dead motherfucker, nigga!"

"You tried that shit already, fool. What, you thought I wouldn't figure out your li'l scheme? Next time, hire some professionals and not some young, dumb pricks to handle your business," Dayvon said.

"This ain't over, you snitchin' faggot. Believe me when I tell you that shit. You know I'ma hit them streets one day real soon. When I do, your ass is mine."

"Yeah, yeah. Bring it, whore. I'm ready for whatever. This DFL squad belongs to me now. Your ass is out. I'm making it official. As a matter of fact, Gena, bring that phat ass over here and let me see you shake that motherfucker. Give Daddy some of that bomb-ass head, like I like it."

Gena switched her sexy ass back over to the bed and stood in front of Dayvon. She leaned her coconut cream-colored ass over so Dayvon could see it jiggle as she danced. She motioned for him to come to the edge of the bed and sit up, then got down on all fours and deep-throated him like she was Janet

Jacme. *Ty's girl got mad skills,* Dayvon thought. She made a slurping sound when her mouth went up and down on his dick. She was loud enough for Ty to hear when Dayvon put the phone down near his crotch.

Ty was dumbfounded. There was nothing worse for a cat in jail than to know that his wifey was fucking another dude while he was doing his bid. It was even worse when it was one of his homeboys. He didn't know which way to turn or what to do at this point. His best friend was now his worst enemy. He had to deal with Li'l Jay and Stink before the cops got to them. His girl had betrayed him in the worst way. He loved the shit outta that girl. He had no one to blame for this whole mess but himself. However, that was a reality he wasn't even trying to hear. He couldn't hit the bricks soon enough to settle the score with Dayvon. After he had heard enough of his baby mama sucking Dayvon off, he hung up the phone. Somebody was getting his ass whipped on the tier that night.

After Dayvon finished screwing Gena, he looked over at her and just laughed to himself. He knew all the while she was fucking with Ty that he could get that pussy. She used to flirt with him when Ty wasn't around, but he never acted on it. Ty was his man, and that would've been breaking the playa's code. When Dayvon used to come by their house to see Ty, Gena would walk around the house half-naked or wearing some tight outfit that showcased her hourglass figure. Gena used to always tell Kiera how sexy Dayvon's lips were and how she wondered if he could eat good pussy. *Stupid bitch should have known Kiera would tell her own brother what she said.* Since Ty wasn't his man no more, he figured he might as well tap that phat ass a few times, just outta spite.

Dayvon was right. Gena had always wanted to get with him. However, it was Ty who stepped to her first that night at the club, D.C. Live. She was with her girls, just soaking in the vibe, when she spotted Ty and Dayvon and their crew spending mad money at the bar. They were buying drinks for all of the ladies. Everybody in B'more and D.C. knew who they were. DFL was a name that was ringing in the streets.

Gena made it her business to be seen by them. She wore a shirt that showed off enough cleavage for her big boobs to be the center of attention. When Ty stepped to her instead of Dayvon, she figured she would still make out all right. They both had no problem spending money on a girl if her hand called for it. She reasoned if she couldn't have the man she wanted, she'd get with his best friend, who was holding just as much loot. Now that she'd had a chance to see what Dayvon's lovin' was like, she was hooked from the first stroke. *Ty who?*

Dayvon had bigger plans for Gena that she had no clue about. Making her his girl was not even an option. How the fuck could he trust a girl who would fuck her son's godfather and her man's business partner? He looked over at her as she slept and took a big toke off his freshly rolled blunt. He had something else, something sinister, in mind that would suit her ass just right. He was becoming as ruthless as Ty and being drawn deeper into the dark side of the game he had tried for so long to avoid. This would make it that much harder for him to walk away from the life.

Pooh's heart was racing as he placed the key in Gena's door. He opened the door quietly and made his way through the house in the silence of the darkness. He knew Manny, Ty's son, wasn't home, so the coast was clear. He wouldn't be able to do his thing if there were kids in the house. That was just one of the rules he lived by.

As he made his way through the house, he observed a series of frames on the walls, containing poems Gena had written. She was a poet and loved to recite her poetry at various spoken word venues across the city. She was also working on a novel about street life. She had read Nikki Turner's book, *A Hustler's Wife,* and figured she could write her own story, based on her life with Ty and the game.

Pooh made his way into the bedroom. He saw Gena and Dayvon lying up in the bed together.

Dayvon acted like he was sleeping, but he was really wide awake. He had gotten up about twenty minutes earlier and flipped the lights in the living room to let Pooh know it was safe to enter the house. As Pooh got closer to the bed he pulled back the covers, exposing the two lovers. He approached Gena and stuck his loaded .45 up against her temple.

"Get up, bitch. Where the fuck is the money at?" he demanded.

Gena was fully alert now. Dayvon tried to act like he was in a state of shock. When Gena realized it was Pooh who was trying to rob her, she couldn't believe her eyes. She didn't know he even knew where she lived. Ty had told her about his beef with Dayvon, but he never mentioned anything about Pooh.

"Pooh, I don't know what money you talkin' about. Ty never keeps money here. Tell him, Dayvon."

"Pooh, calm down, kid. What the fuck you doin' this for? You want money? I can get that for you. You ain't even gotta go out like this," Dayvon said. He was playing his part to perfection.

"Fuck that shit. I want the money now. I know it's here. Somebody better start kicking it out or I'ma start splitting wigs up in here!" Pooh said angrily. He wrapped his finger around the trigger and forced the barrel of his gun into Gena's mouth to let her know he wasn't playing. Gena was terrified. Her body was trembling and tears started pouring from her eyes. Gena was a hard chick, but there's something about a loaded pistol in your mouth that could bring out the scared little kid in anybody.

"Gena, just tell him where the safe is. Give him the money so he can get what he came for. I ain't tryin'a die over no bullshit like this," Dayvon interjected.

"Okay, okay. Shit. Just give me a minute to throw some clothes on," she responded.

Gena couldn't believe Dayvon was being so calm in a situation like this. That was when she realized he had set her up. She knew no one but Dayvon knew about Ty's safe. There was over $500,000 in there. It was all of Ty's money she had been saving throughout the years. She was the only one except Ty with the combination. As she got up to put on her clothes, she noticed Pooh was staring at her naked frame like a hungry vulture eyeing a fresh piece of meat. She made her way into the closet to get to the safe. Pooh kept his pistol pointed at her the whole time. She punched in the code to open the safe then began placing the neatly stacked piles of $100 bills into the sack Pooh had given her.

After she finished taking out the money and exited the closet, she looked over at Dayvon. He was wearing a grin on his face as wide as could be.

"Dayvon, how the fuck could you do this to me?" she asked.

"It's business, never personal, sweetie. Thanks for the good times, baby," he responded. She was crying and pleading for her life, but it was to no avail.

"Come on, y'all. You got the money. Think about my son. I'm all he's got."

"Well, if you're all he's got, then shorty ain't got shit to look forward to. You is a triflin' ho, fuckin' his godfather. A ho like you is the worst kinda bitch. You make kids turn out like me," Pooh said. He squeezed the trigger twice.

Gena's body fell limp across the bed as the two bullets pierced her skull. She never got a chance to feel any pain. The life was sucked from her body and her blood soaked the sheets. The neighbors didn't hear a sound because of the silencer Pooh had used on his gun.

Dayvon got up and put on his clothes. They removed any evidence of their presence in the house. The scene looked like another drug-related robbery gone bad. These kinds of cases gave the police a fit because they usually went unsolved.

Dayvon and Pooh exited quietly through the back door. They got away with Ty's money, splitting it 50/50. This was only the beginning of what they had in store for Ty.

# 12
# The Gift and the Curse

"Where the heck are my shoes?" Cheri asked herself.

She was maneuvering about her exquisite condo, trying to get dressed to make it on time for her appointment. The mad rush in the morning was an everyday ritual she had yet to get used to. Trying to find the right outfit to match with the right shoes was a meaningful task for this glamour girl. After she found the right ensemble, she had to decide which scent she felt like wearing that day. She had a selection of perfume and scented lotions that would put both Bath and Body Works and Macy's to shame. She decided on her Aqua di Gio perfume because of its light yet attractive scent. She looked through her collection of silver jewelry to find the perfect earring and bracelet set to complete her look.

After all the hoopla of getting dressed was resolved, Cheri looked fly as could be in her sundress, which accented every curve of her voluptuous figure. She was a sure 'nuff brick house. She wore her hair out and let it flow freely, because it had grown in length over the last few months. It was now down to the middle of her back. Her nails were manicured and feet pedicured, painted with a design that complemented her outfit. She found her sandals and quickly slid them onto her feet. Her toes were so petite and sexy that any man would pay a pretty penny to suck on each one, individually, just to savor the flavor.

As she prepared to leave her house, she had to turn around and make a quick beeline to the bathroom because of her upset stomach. She hadn't been able to retain any solid foods for days. As she raised her head away from the toilet bowl, her eyes were watery and she felt light-headed. Touching her forehead, she noticed she had a fever and slight case of the chills. She had been feeling this way for the last week or so. She had finally decided to go see her doctor to find out what was wrong with her.

Cheri sat on the edge of her bed for a few minutes in an effort to regain her balance. She made her way back to the bathroom to brush her teeth to get rid of the smell of vomit on her breath. Feeling better, she managed to gather the strength to try to leave her house again.

When she opened her front door, the brightness of the sun almost blinded her. She threw on her Coco Chanel shades and proceeded. The weather in Georgia was always beautiful in the summertime. The flowers and the leaves on the trees were in full bloom. She could feel a slight morning breeze just cool enough to offset the humidity in the air. It had rained the night before, but the warm night air had sucked up the fallen water and made it appear as though it had never fallen from the sky.

Cheri made her way down the sidewalk toward her car, which was sitting in her reserved space. She fumbled through her purse for the keys to her convertible Beamer. When she found them, she pressed the button on her alarm to unlock the doors.

Her car looked clean enough to eat off the hood. Cheri took her car to get washed and detailed at least twice a week. She made sure she kept it showroom floor sparkling. Everything about Ms. Cheri Jackson just said she was a top-notch business executive. This sistah was definitely on the move, with a limitless future.

Driving down the highway, she sang along with the vocal stylings of Vivian Green as her latest single, "Emotional Rollercoaster," played on the radio. It got her thinking about Dayvon and the relationship between them.

She had it bad for him, and no matter how hard she tried to fight it, she couldn't get him off her mind. Every night she lay awake in her bed, longing to feel his firm hands caress her flesh and to gaze at his handsome face, soaking in every fine detail. She loved his thuggish ways. They made her feel secure when he was around. A corporate type of brotha just didn't do it for her. Dayvon's lovemaking quenched her every sexual desire—so much so that it made her naïve to the reality of their relationship.

In her mind, they were in a committed, long-distance relationship. She accepted the fact that she only saw him for maybe one week out of every month. She had visited him in Baltimore three times over the past year, but more often he came to see her.

When she was in his hometown, he treated her like a queen. She hadn't noticed any other girls calling him when they were together. She didn't know Dayvon had turned his phone off and would check his messages whenever she went to the bathroom.

Dayvon told Cheri he used to sell drugs, but he'd stopped about two years before. He told her he owned several stores around the city and that was why he was always so busy. He never mentioned having other women in his life to her, but then again, she never asked. She just trusted what he said about his business ventures limiting the amount of time they could spend together. Over time, she hoped things would improve and he would be able to see her more often.

Cheri was just doing what so many women in love do; she was rationalizing the most irrational circumstances and situations. She didn't want to see the insanity of her thinking and actions when the painful and real picture was clear to everyone else.

It had been almost two weeks since she talked to Dayvon on the phone. The last time she saw him was right after Jaré's shooting. He made no plans with her to come back to Atlanta anytime soon. She left him numerous messages and he had yet to call her back.

Cheri missed him more and more with each passing day. She turned down the volume a little on her radio and retrieved her cell phone from her purse. She was determined to reach her man. As she dialed his number, she popped in her Alicia Keys CD. She skipped to track number three, which was a remake of the Prince classic, "How Come U Don't Call Me Anymore?" She wanted it playing in the background for him to hear. The underlying message would be obvious. A blind man could see this girl was wide open for Dayvon. Once again, she got no answer, so she left a message.

"Yeah, baby. It's me again. I know you're busy handlin' yours right now. I just wanted to let you know I was thinking about you. I wanna see you as soon as possible. I got some new toys the other day that we can play with. Mommy's kitten is purring for you to come stroke her like only you can. I got an itch I need you to scratch. Anyway, call me back. Love you, boo."

She hung up the phone. This was the first time those words had flowed from her lips arid she made her true feelings known to Dayvon. She awaited his response to her startling revelation.

"Ms. Jackson, the doctor will see you now," the nurse said. Cheri had waited almost a half hour for her name to be called. Doctor Day was late finishing up her prior appointment.

As Cheri walked toward the swinging door, Dr. Day greeted her with a warm smile. She was an elegantly beautiful black woman in her mid 50's. She was classy and chic, like Lena Horne. She walked with a style and grace that let you know she was all that and a bag of chips. Dr. Day had been Cheri's primary doctor since she was ten years old. She was a close friend of Cheri's mother, almost like an extended member of the family.

"So, sweetie, how is your mother doing? I haven't heard from her in a few weeks. How is the rest of the family?" she asked Cheri.

"They're all doing fine. In fact, my mother told me to tell you to call her. She wants to do lunch with you later in the week," Cheri responded.

"I sure will do that. So, what brings you here today?"

"I've been feeling kinda faint lately and throwing up a lot. I can't eat anything. At night, I get the chills and I wake up in a cold sweat. It's like I have the flu or some type of summer cold."

"How long have you been feeling this way?"

"About a week or so."

"All right. Let's run a few tests so we can see what's going on. It's probably nothing serious."

Dr. Day gave Cheri a routine physical exam. All of her vital signs were normal, but her temperature was a little high, just above 100 degrees. She also noticed the glands on Cheri's neck were a little swollen. That wasn't uncommon to have with a cold. Cheri had lost almost seven pounds since her last physical, though it was hardly noticeable because of her thickly built physique.

Dr. Day took urine and blood samples and sent them to the lab to be tested. The blood work would take about a week to come back, but the urine results would be back momentarily. She instructed Cheri to wait in the lobby for her urine results and to schedule an appointment for the following week to get her blood test results.

A short while later, Dr. Day called Cheri back into the office. She informed her that her urine results had come back and showed no abnormalities. She gave Cheri some antibiotics, just in case it was a cold or the flu causing her ailment, and said she hoped she felt better soon.

Tears stained Cheri's face a week later as she ran from the doctor's office. She couldn't believe the news she had just received from Dr. Day. Not only was she pregnant, but she was also HIV positive—a gift and a curse. What more could one person go through in the same day? Her emotions didn't allow her to stay around and receive medical advice from the doctor. She was dumbfounded. Her perfect world had been turned upside down.

As she sat in her car, flashes of her life appeared before her eyes. She was in a delusional state, on the verge of losing her mind. *How did this happen? Who gave it to me? How can I tell my family the news? What did I do to deserve such a sad twist of fate? Will my baby be born into the world with HIV? Am I going to die?* All of these questions and many more were racing through her head. She pulled herself together just enough to be able to drive home.

On her way home, she ran down her list of recent lovers and only two men came to mind. One was her ex, Larry. They had broken up right before she met Dayvon. The last time they had sex was around that same time. She hadn't heard from him since. She was sure he would have told her if he had such a serious disease. They had a long history together and she was confident in that fact.

Then there was Dayvon. She knew this was his baby, because he was the only one she was sleeping with recently. Now she was starting to ask herself the questions she should have asked a long time ago. *Does he have another woman, or several, back in Baltimore? Would he tell me if he was positive? How well do I really know this man?*

She came to the conclusion quickly that it had to be him who had given her this disease. She was filled with rage. She was determined to make him pay for her ill fate. The seeds of revenge were growing inside her by the minute.

When she pulled up to her condo, she parked her car in its assigned spot. She sat in her car for a few minutes before letting out a piercing scream in frustration. The loud noise frightened several of her neighbors. They ran to their windows to see what the commotion was. They thought someone had been attacked. What they saw was the shattered shell of a woman as she ran into her house. She was searching for answers to unanswerable questions; she was looking for someone to unleash her wrath upon. Cheri closed her front door and was left alone to ponder her uncertain future.

# 13
# Money on My Mind

Nikki had stopped by for a quickie before she went to work. She was giving that pussy to me like she never had before. She wasn't even stressing that I had to wear a condom anymore. That was fine with me, because it made the sex that much better. She hadn't given me any diseases thus far. She was on the pill, so her getting pregnant wasn't even an issue. I knew she had a boyfriend, but I didn't care. He never stood in the way of me hittin' that ass when I wanted. She was my part-time lover, but she was his full-time problem.

I was pounding her pussy from the back, grabbing her braids. She was begging me to long-stroke that big ass. As I was going in and out of her, she tightened up the walls of her pussy to put more pressure on my dick. I loved it when she did that, because it added extra friction. She let me know I was hitting the right spots when she pulled me closer to her and started screaming my name. Nikki was the vocal type and she loved for me to call her a nasty, stinkin', slutty bitch when we fucked. It was something about them words that excited her in the heat of passion. When I was ready to release, I turned her over and came all over her face. That drove her wild to see me let out a big explosion like that.

After I came, I relaxed on the bed and enjoyed her little show. She started playing with her pussy, making herself have orgasm after orgasm. The more she rubbed her clit, the hotter she got. When she finally let the big one go, she squirted pussy juice all over the sheets. Her orgasm was bigger than mine. It's every man's fantasy to see a girl cum like that, at least once in his lifetime. After she was finished, she got up, took a shower, got dressed, and was off to work. A little while later I was ready to bounce because I had business to tend to that day.

Pooh was late as hell. I took out my cell phone to call him to see why. It was unlike him. I couldn't get mad with shorty, though, because he was my eyes and ears out in the streets. He held things down for me while I was laying low. Pooh was mad mature to be so young. I guess that came from growing up in the streets and having to be the sole provider for his family. He was a smart kid. He had the potential to do a lot of positive things with his life if he left the thug life alone. All the arrests on his record were juvenile charges. He didn't have to worry about them coming back to haunt him for the rest of his years. He could easily go to college and become a doctor or lawyer or some shit. I was gonna holla at him about getting outta the game once we finished with Ty. However, for right now, I needed his services for another purpose.

"Damn, nigga. Where the hell you at? It's ten-thirty. You was supposed to be here a half hour ago. Let me find out Dina got you tied up in some freaky shit you can't get out of," I said to him when he answered the phone.

"Nah, dog. I just had to tie up a few loose ends. Don't sweat it, though. It ain't nothing I can't handle. I'ma be there in like ten minutes," he responded.

"I'll be out front."

"Holla."

Ever since we'd done that job on Gena, things had gone a little crazy. Pooh said the cops were getting hip to the fact that drama was brewing between me and Ty. They had raided all of our stash houses. They didn't find anything, but Ronnie-O got popped. They caught him with two ounces of coke in his ride. His bail was set at $50,000. I would have to send somebody to bail him out. I couldn't afford to have one of my lieutenants locked down and not pull him. There was also a chance Ty could get to him behind bars, since he was riding with me.

Li'l Jay and Stink were on the run since it was all over the news and in the papers that they were involved in the shooting of Jaré and Sasha. They could run, but they had to show their faces at some point in time. It was in their best interests if the cops got to them before I did.

Kiera called and told me the police came by my parents' house looking for me. They wanted to question me about Gena's death. I knew they had been trying to build a racketeering case against us for years, but we always managed to outsmart them. They couldn't find me, because none of my cribs were in my real name. I always paid my rent up front, in cash. When your money was long like mine, you could always find someone to rent to you with no questions asked.

I was sitting on the steps of my condo when Pooh pulled up in his platinum-colored Navigator.

"What up, D? Where that phat ass Nikki at?" he asked.

"She left an hour ago. Why you clocking my hoes, fool? Don't you got enough of your own?"

"I'm just saying, dog. When you finish with her ass, pass her on to me. I'ma show her how it feels to be with a real man."

"Whatever, nigga. Your game is tight, but you still got a few years to catch up with me, son. Remember that," I told him then playfully popped him upside his head. He was the little brother I never had. I could see he wanted to follow in my footsteps.

"So, what's poppin'?" I asked him.

"Five-O been sweating me lately. They trying hard to bag you, Day. They was tailing my ass to get to you, but I lost them back on 295. They can't hold me when I'm behind the wheel. I'm like Mario Andretti behind this motherfucker," he said. We both busted out laughing.

"That's my li'l nigga. I knew there was a reason why I fucked with you. So, when they hit your spot the other day, what happened?" I asked.

"Nothing much. You know the drill. Po-po did a sweep and grabbed the youngstas up and tried to shake 'em down. Everybody was clean, as usual. Your man Danny looked out once again. The only thing was I couldn't get in touch with Ronnie-O in time to give him a heads up. It was my bad that he got knocked," he said.

Danny Witherspoon was a friend I had grown up with in Randallstown. He had become a Baltimore narcotics officer. He tipped us off whenever the police were planning to raid one of our spots. I, of course, compensated him well for his information. In this game, one hand had to wash the other. If there was no crime, then there would be no need for police officers. If people weren't getting high, then I couldn't make any money. We all needed each other to keep the cycle in constant rotation.

"Have you been through the Heights to pick up that loot from Sammy and Mark?" I asked. Sammy and Mark had stepped up and taken over Li'l Jay and Stink's crews.

"Yeah, their money was on point," he said. He reached underneath his seat and pulled out a knapsack. It was filled with money. There had to be at least a hundred grand in there. I gave him twenty-five grand to keep for himself. The rest was going with me to my lawyer's office to be washed clean.

"We gotta get somebody over there to bail Ronnie-O out," I said.

"It's already taken care of. I sent JD to do that this morning."

"You on point, Pooh. I gotta watch your li'l ass. You might come for my spot one day."

"Nah, D. We family. You looked out for me when I needed it. I'm just returning the favor."

"It's all love, kid. Pull over there in the parking lot. Wait right here for me while I run in here to handle this business real quick," I instructed.

I jumped out of the truck and walked across the street. I made my way through the crowd of pedestrians, into the USF&G building. My business lawyer, Marty Weinstein, had an office on the seventh floor in there. I checked in with the security officer at the front desk and got a pass to go upstairs to his office. When I got off the elevator and made my way down the hall to Marty's office, I was greeted at the door by Marty's secretary. Gretchen was a fine German chick with long, blond hair that came all the way down to her slender but firm ass.

"How are you doing today, Mr. Freeman?" she asked.

"I'm doing good. Is your boss with a client or one of his female associates?" I asked her playfully.

Marty was a slick Jewish dude who could never be mistaken for humble. He was in his late 50's and dressed sharp as a tack in his tailor-made Italian suits. He had a charismatic personality that went over well with the ladies. He was the epitome of an old school playa. He had no wife, no kids, and no attachments. However, he did have a phone book full of female friends. He especially liked black women. He said he preferred his women with some meat on their bones.

His philandering ways were no secret around his office. That was why I could joke with Gretchen about him the way I did. He and I always joked with each other about the drama we had with the women in our lives. On top of that, he made me a lot of money with his investment schemes. He made my dirty money look so fresh and so clean.

"No, he's not with anyone. He's expecting you. He'll be right out." She buzzed him to let him know I was in the lobby. I was checking out Gretchen's backside as she came from behind the desk and walked over to the copy machine. Nice view. About five minutes later, Marty walked out of his office.

"Dayvon, my man. What's up? Long time, no see," he said. He was just too cool for me. We shook hands and walked into his office to parlay.

"Life is getting hectic, Marty. Tell me some good news," I said to him.

"Yeah, Mark has been telling me about your potential legal woes," he said. He was referring to Mark Rubinstein, my legal attorney. Mark and Marty had been friends since college.

Mark was the reason the police and I hadn't had many conversations throughout the years. He had won a rack of cases for some of my workers to keep them out of jail, and he had a lot of pull down at the courthouse. As a matter of fact, if Ty had let Mark defend him, he could have made his case disappear. Instead, his stupid ass got his own lawyer and wound up serving time.

"Yeah, but I'ma be a'ight. So, what's up with my money?" I asked.

"I hope you're all right, kid. You're a good guy; I like you. You're not a knucklehead like your boy Ty. You got a good head on your shoulders. I don't wanna see anything bad happen to you.

"As far as your money goes, your profit margins are going through the roof. You have a net worth of almost five million dollars. You need to take this money and get the hell outta Baltimore now. Go somewhere far away and start a new life. Don't let the streets rob you of your best years," he said. His words struck a chord with me. We were on the same page.

"Marty, you're reading my mind. As soon as I take care of a few loose ends, I'm outta here. I'm going somewhere nice and warm where I can start a new life." I handed him the bag of money Pooh had given me. "I need you to find a way to transfer my money when I decide where I'm going. Here goes another stack for you to flip for me. Put it into one of those accounts I set up for my sister," I said.

"Say no more, kid. Just tell me where and when."

I liked Marty. Even though our relationship was mainly business, I could see his concern was genuine. Since he didn't have any children of his own, I think he had grown to look at me like a son. Most people say all lawyers are shady, but he always played fair with me.

He ran down the specifics of my accounts to me so I could see where my money was going. After I was satisfied with what I heard, I jetted out of his office and back to the parking lot to meet Pooh.

"Is everything good, D?" Pooh asked.

"It's all good, son. Let's get the fuck outta downtown. It's too hot for me to be out here in the public for too long," I said.

"You got that. Now, what about Li'l Jay and Stink? I got a call while you was gone. I know where to find Li'l Jay. Let me get his ass for you. I wanna break him off something real proper. When I tell you the deal, you gonna flip," he said.

"Handle yours, son. Just be careful and watch your back. Let me know when you find his ass. First, though, shoot me out to Ellicott City to my crib so I can chill for a few," I said.

Pooh pulled off and made his way onto Martin Luther King Boulevard, going toward I-95. About twenty-five minutes later, we pulled up at my place. He went inside first to make sure it was safe for me to go in there. After he saw that everything was cool, he bounced. He was on a mission to find Li'l Jay. Knowing Pooh, he wouldn't rest until that motherfucker's eyes were closed for good.

# 14
# Puttin' In Work

The weekends were always jumping in the Baltimore/D.C. area. The clubs were always packed to capacity. In Baltimore, spots like Club Choices or Club One were the places to go if you were looking for the jump off. In the P.G. County/D.C. area, there was Crossroads, VIP, and Dreams to get your party on. Pooh and his crew were regulars at one of these spots every weekend. On any Friday or Saturday night, you might find him, Tyrell, Shawn, and Shady Mike holding court at any of these clubs. As a part of the DFL family, they got VIP treatment and the pick of the litter of all the baddest bitches wherever they went.

This foursome had been hanging together since junior high school. Pooh and Tyrell were first cousins on Pooh's father's side. Even though Pooh's father wasn't a part of his life, he and Tyrell wound up attending the same schools and developing a close-knit bond. Everyone knew they were related because they had similar facial features and the same slender build.

Shawn lived three doors up from Pooh on Wildwood Parkway in the Village, and he was Dina's twin brother. Even though his sister was Pooh's main girl, that didn't stop Shawn from chasing pussy with Pooh on a regular basis. What they did together was none of his sister's business, he reasoned.

Shawn stood about 6 feet 4 inches tall and 200-plus pounds, with rippling muscles. He could easily be mistaken for a bouncer in any nightclub. That was why he served as an enforcer for the family whenever somebody's count came up short or a junkie needed a beatdown.

Finally, Shady Mike was a cat they added to the crew because of his resourcefulness. He got his name because of his shifty eyes and the numerous credit card and check scams he ran outside the drug game. If someone wanted the latest gear, a new TV, DVD player, or anything before it hit the stores, then he was the man to see.

The four of them were the best of friends and held down the tightest crew in the DFL family for sure.

"Yo, so where we going tonight?" Shawn asked.

"It don't matter to me, dog, as long as there's some fine bitches and a lotta liquor there. But on the real, let's go out to Dreams. I feel like fuckin' with some of them sophisticated P.G. County hoes tonight," Tyrell said. Mike nodded in agreement.

"Nah, yo. We gotta do something local. I'm waiting on a call later on. We gotta be nearby so we can handle this business, ya know. Let's do Choices tonight," Pooh said. He was their leader, so everybody usually went along with his decision.

Everybody's gear was tight. All of their jewels were shining bright, emitting a sparkling glare from the ice on their DFL platinum chains and Rolex watches. Pooh, Tyrell, and Mike had just gotten fresh haircuts earlier in the day at Perfect Images Barbershop on Mulberry Street. Shawn had his girl, Maria, tighten up his cornrows that morning. Dayvon made it mandatory for his top soldiers to always represent the fam with class.

As the blunt was being passed around and Mary J. Blige's new joint with Method Man was blasting out of Tyrell's spankin' new Cadillac Escalade, they pulled into a parking spot on Charles Street, a few feet away from the club. They all jumped out of the truck and proceeded toward the club. A long line of Baltimore's finest ghetto hotties stood before them as they made their way past the line to the front door. They never waited in line anywhere they went. They could see the hate and jealousy in the eyes of all the cats in line as they were escorted by security into the club.

As they walked through the crowd and made their way to the bar, everybody was scanning the crop of females, looking for new victims. Pooh and Tyrell were the smooth ones in the crew, so they usually set things up with the ladies for Mike and Shawn. They always had the right line at the right time for the right female to make her want to give up the panties. Pooh had an added advantage with his green eyes, and he had learned a lot throughout the years, watching Dayvon break so many women down.

On the other hand, Mike was clever when it came to running schemes and gettin' money, but when it came down to the ladies, he had no game and his rap was so weak. Shawn had a bad habit of stuttering real heavy, and it got worse whenever he tried to talk to a fine girl in front of a crowd of people. The thing about this crew was whenever one of them got some ass, everybody had to get some ass.

When they reached the bar, they ordered several bottles of Hypnotiq and Cristal to get the night started. It would be nothing but the best for these young stars.

"Yo, Pooh, look at shorty over there. She been checking you out since we came in the door. Go see what's up with her and her crew," Shawn said. He was talking about four fine dime pieces ordering drinks at the other end of the bar. The chocolate-complexioned honey was checking out Pooh in particular.

"No doubt, kid. I'ma handle that. I'ma show you how it's done," Pooh said. Shawn was right on point with this one, because he knew Pooh liked his women dark and lovely. Pooh took a sip of the

Hypnotiq and made his way over to the other end of the bar.

"Excuse me, ladies. My name is Tamir, but you can call me Pooh. I don't mean to interrupt y'all parlayin' over here, but I was wondering if I could speak to your girl here in private if you don't mind," he said in his smoothest tone. He looked sexual chocolate in her eyes to let her know he was talking about her. Her body language let him know she was feeling him too.

"Ummm, nice to meet you, Pooh. The name is Sharonda. Anything you want to say to me, you can say in front of my girls. This is Chantel, Mona, and Jazel. We roll like that," she responded. She knew who he was already; his name was ringing in the streets as the next young don. She tried to play it cool to let him know her game was just as tight.

"Lovely Sharonda, no doubt. I can respect that. Well, I was wondering what you were drinking because I was gonna tell the bartender to put it on my tab. The same goes for your girls, too. Next, I was gonna ask you to dance. Or are you gonna have me wondering all night if you can move as good as you look standing over here? Finally, my boys over there are getting kinda lonely at the other of the bar and they'd like to meet your girls. Let's make that happen," he said. He knew his game was on point, and that's why he spoke with such confidence.

"Well, Mr. Tamir, to answer your questions in order, you can order us all Apple Martinis. Next, yeah, we can hit the dance floor so I can see what you working with. Finally, as for my girls hooking up with your boys, we can let them handle that while we go do our thing," she said. She grabbed Pooh by the hand and led him to the dance floor for some hardcore bumpin' and grindin'.

Her girls made their way over to the other end of the bar to holla at Tyrell and the rest of Pooh's crew. They were just as fine as Sharonda in their body-huggin' outfits, made to get attention. Each one of them had already checked out Pooh's boys and knew which one of the guys they were gonna holla at. Sharonda and her girls were some bonafide gold diggers. If Pooh and them were down to kick out the cash, then everybody was getting laid tonight. For the next hour or two, everybody got drunk as hell and had a good time until Pooh got the phone call he had been waiting for.

Pooh stepped away from the rest of the gang to handle his business. After he finished his call, he gathered up his troops. He told the ladies they had to make a quick run, but they could all hook up later that night to finish the party at the Hyatt downtown. Sharonda and her girls were all too with it to roll with a group of ballas. Pooh peeled off a roll of hundred dollar bills and gave them to Sharonda to pay for renting the hotel's penthouse suite. She gave him her cell phone number so he could call her once they were finished running their errand. Everybody exchanged hugs and Pooh and his crew left the club while Sharonda and her squad continued to get their party on.

After they left the club, everybody changed from their club clothes into black jeans and black hooded sweatshirts. It was time to put in work, and they needed to be dressed for the occasion. They parked Tyrell's truck a couple of blocks away from the club and jumped into an old Chevy Nova they used to carry out jobs like the one they had planned. Going to the club was just a diversion to create an alibi for the mission they had to carry out that night. Sharonda and her crew were an added bonus for them for later on. Nobody could argue with the fact that they had four fine-ass witnesses to verify their whereabouts. Pooh knew that if he gave Sharonda and her girls a nice chunk of cash they could easily be convinced to say they were all together for the entire night, even after the club was closed. That being said, they had two hours to accomplish their mission and make their way downtown to the hotel.

"Yo, where the hell is this house at?" Tyrell asked. They were somewhere in the Mount Vernon area of the city.

"Bootsie said it's the house on the corner with the red light on," Pooh answered. He pointed out a house that appeared to be the one they were looking for. He checked the address; it was the right house. He instructed Tyrell to park the car around the corner.

"A'ight, this is it, y'all. Everybody knows what they gotta do. I want this job to be tight with no mistakes. We in and out in ten minutes," Pooh said to his boys.

"We got you, nigga. I just can't believe this shit. Dayvon is gonna laugh his ass off about this one. If he only knew what kinda niggas we had working with us," Mike said, trying to suppress his laughter.

"Yo, this ain't no joke, fool. Get serious. We can laugh about this shit later on," Tyrell said. He was always tight-faced when it was time to put in work, because he believed in carrying out a job to perfection. He didn't want anyone joking around at a time like this. That was how mistakes got made.

"My bad, dog. I was just fucking around," Mike said in return.

Over the last year or so, Bootsie had become one of Pooh's biggest customers. He would buy ounces of coke from Pooh every week. His money was always right on time. Bootsie and his friends loved to get high by free-basing cocaine or speedballing it with heroin. The fact that he was a transvestite didn't matter to Pooh. As long as he had money to spend, they could do business.

Bootsie stood about 5 feet 10 inches tall and had a muscular build from working out, but he could easily pass for a woman with his curvy figure. His outer appearance was all woman because he kept his hair and nails done to a T. His breast implants had fooled many straight dudes throughout the years. He was a favorite prostitute to many so-called thugs who came home from jail and still had an urge for some jailhouse ass to fuck. If anybody knew about a so-called straight dude who was in the closet, it was Bootsie.

Pooh learned not to pay his strange ways any mind, because Bootsie was a regular customer and always brought him new ones who spent just as much money as he did. Plus, Bootsie was willing to drop a dime on somebody for a little extra coke in his package. He kept his ears and eyes open to everything that went down in the streets. That's why when he called Pooh a couple days before with some info, Pooh jumped at the opportunity to see if it was legit or not.

As Pooh, Shawn, and Mike made their way toward the house, everybody put on their ski masks to conceal their identities. It was so quiet outside you could hear a pin drop. They walked slowly up the block, being sure not to make any noise to draw attention to themselves at such a late hour. When they got to the front door, Pooh reached for the doorknob. When he turned it, the door opened just as Bootsie said it would. Bootsie had two roommates, but he told Pooh he would be alone with one of his favorite clients that night.

The trio made their way through the house and up the stairs toward the master bedroom. You could hear loud moans and groans coming from the far end of the hall. Bootsie was getting his freak on tonight with a very happy customer.

When they cracked open the door, none of them were prepared for the sight before their eyes. It was Li'l Jay, getting fucked doggy style by Bootsie, and he appeared to be enjoying himself. Bootsie was also slapping Jay in the face with a dildo. The lovers apparently didn't hear the door open, because they were going at it nonstop. The trio just stood there with their jaws on the floor, in a state of shock.

"Damn, that shit feels good, baby. Put it in deeper," Li'l Jay said.

"Shut up, bitch. I want you to suck this dick," Bootsie said to him. He pulled himself outta Jay's ass and stuck his erect penis in Jay's mouth. Li'l Jay began sucking Bootsie off like he was a sure 'nuff pro. After a moment of watching Jay do his thing, Pooh couldn't take it anymore. He pulled out his gun and busted the door wide open.

"Nigga, get your faggot ass up. So, I see you like to take it up the ass, huh?" he shouted. Pooh took off his mask so Jay could see him. Jay jumped up and almost shitted on himself. He couldn't say a word because he was straight busted. His secret was out in the open.

Bootsie had told Pooh that for the last three years, Jay and Stink had been regular customers for him and his friends. He said they started off just getting blowjobs. They would insist they weren't gay because they weren't getting fucked or penetrating a man. Over time, though, one thing led to another and both of them started coming down to Mount Vernon on a regular basis to trick. Curiosity had gotten the best of them, and all of their inhibitions went out the window. Bootsie said they were so strung out he would fuck one or both of them at least three times a week. Jay had even talked about moving in with him. When Bootsie found out about the reward on the streets for info on the whereabouts of either one of them, he was only too eager to share what he knew with Pooh, his favorite drug dealer.

"Oh, shit. Yo, this ain't what you think it is. Let me explain," Jay said. He knew his fate was all but sealed. He was about to die in a shameful way.

"What you gotta explain, fool? Get your punk ass up. Oh, don't even think about putting no clothes on," Mike said as he took off his mask to reveal his identity also.

"Bitch, you set me up. I should kill your ass!" Jay said to Bootsie as he lunged toward him. Bootsie jumped up, scared as hell. Before Jay could reach Bootsie, Shawn and Mike grabbed him by the ankles and dragged him off the bed. They tied up his arms and feet and duct taped his mouth then carried his naked body down the stairs. Jay tried to resist, but his efforts were in vain. He was caught with his pants down, literally.

"Nigga, if you even think about making any noise when we get outside, I'ma make your death even more slow and painful than I planned to," Pooh said. He ran back up the stairs to the bedroom to give Bootsie the five grand he had promised for the info. Plus, he gave him an overflowing sandwich bag full of cocaine as an added bonus for his help.

"Good looking out. If you find out anything about that other fool let me know. You ain't gotta worry about this shit coming back on you. Trust me," Pooh said. He knew Bootsie would keep his mouth shut.

"Thanks, Pooh. You do keep your word. That surely makes a girl like me happy," Bootsie said as he closed his robe. He was messing with Pooh. He knew Pooh wasn't gay, but he was cool enough with him that Pooh didn't take his little joke seriously. Pooh exited the room and made his way back downstairs to finish up the job.

Pooh opened the front door as Mike and Shawn carried Jay's soon-to-be-dead body down the street toward the car. Tyrell had stayed in the car because he was supposed to be the getaway driver. He got out and popped the trunk. Shawn and Mike stuffed Jay's body in. Once they had him secure in the trunk, they all jumped into the car and made their way across town to their next destination.

"So, where the fuck is your boy at?" Dayvon asked as he burned Jay once again with the butt of his cigarette. Jay screamed in pain. No one would hear his cries; they were in the basement of one of the many abandoned houses in West Baltimore they used to torture motherfuckers. The next occupied house was about three blocks away.

"I ain't telling you shit. Fuck you, nigga. If you gonna kill me, get it over with," Jay said. Tears of pain were welling up in his eyes.

"Nah, nigga, you was supposed to be the next big man out in these streets. You shoulda known I was gonna catch on to your bitch ass. Ty put y'all up to knockin' my girl off. Well, he gonna get the same thing you about to get, but much worse. Fuckin' homo thug. Y'all bitches killed my seed. I'ma ask you one more time. Where the fuck is your boy at?" Dayvon yelled.

"Fuck you. I'ma see you in hell, motherfucker," Jay said. He knew his life was about to end. Pooh and Tyrell took turns burning him with cigarette butts. They poured rubbing alcohol on his burns to further intensify his pain.

"Fine. If that's how you want it, then that's how it's gonna be. Since you like taking it up the ass,

I got a special treat for you," Dayvon said. He greased up the barrel of his nine and stuck it up Jay's ass, shoving it in and out in a rugged manner. Jay winced in pain as the cold steel left its lasting impression on his anal walls.

"You like how that feels, pussy boy? Is it good to you? This is gonna be the last time you get to feel something hot and warm up in there," Dayvon said as he squeezed the trigger. Jay's bloody insides spilled all over the floor. He was slowly bleeding to death.

Pooh and the rest of his gang stood in the back of the basement in a state of shock. They had never seen this side of Dayvon. After Jay squirmed and grunted in pain for a while, he breathed his last breath. The smirk on Dayvon's face let them know he was enjoying the sight of Jay's excruciatingly painful demise.

"Take this as a lesson, my niggas. This is what happens to turncoat motherfuckers. Clean this shit up."

Mike and Shawn wrapped Jay's lifeless body and spilled insides in a large rug. They cleaned up all visible traces of blood and made sure no evidence of their presence in the house was left behind. As they carried his corpse up the stairs and to the car, everybody was silent. They put the body in the trunk and Tyrell sped off. They planned to dump the body out in Lincoln Park, where the remains of so many bodies from a string of unsolved murders in Baltimore could be found.

After they dumped the body, Pooh, Shawn, Mike and Tyrell made it back to Tyrell's truck to change into their club clothes. Their next stop would be the after party at the hotel with Sharonda and her crew. Dayvon jumped into his Lexus SUV and slowly cruised away into the night. He didn't give a second thought to the brutal murder he had just committed.

# 15
# Upside Down, Inside Out

No matter how hard I tried to deny it to myself, I had been longing to feel Dayvon's strong hands all over my body for quite some time. When he ran his fingers through my hair, it sent a chill up my spine and my thighs began to tremble. My nipples were at full attention as he slowly sucked and teased them with his warm, moist tongue. His steamy kisses on the back of my neck made my toes curl in sheer ecstasy. I hadn't felt this kind of passion in a long while.

I lost all control when he inserted three fingers into my pussy and fucked me at a rapid pace. My body went into convulsions with every thrust of his hand. He stuck his tongue in my mouth to try to muffle my loud screams of passion, but it was to no avail. He pulled his hand from between my thighs and inserted his fingers in his mouth to taste my love juice.

"Damn, Jaré. It's been a long time. You taste so sweet. Tell Daddy what you want me to do to you," Dayvon said.

"Oooh, papi. I want you to fuck the shit outta me. But first, let me taste you inside my mouth," I said as I caught a glimpse of his throbbing member.

Dayvon granted my wish. He leaned back on the bed and allowed me to climb between his legs. He always liked me to get up close and personal with his hard love muscle. I started nibbling on his neck and sucking on his earlobes, then I moved farther south and kissed his masculine chest, playfully biting his nipples. I worked my way slowly down below his waist and took all of him into my mouth. I slid up and down his shaft with my tongue, savoring every bit of the flavor. Dayvon's eyes were about to roll into the back of his head. When he couldn't contain himself any longer, he released himself into my mouth and I swallowed every drop of his cum.

"I ain't finished with this dick yet, nigga. I wanna feel you in each and every way tonight," I said.

We engaged in erotic foreplay for about ten minutes before Dayvon's manhood was back up to the task. He got on top of me, spread my legs as wide as the sea and placed himself inside of me. I couldn't describe the good feeling in words, but his nonstop, rhythmic humpin' told me he felt right at home making love to me. I was screaming at the top of my lungs for him to put it in all the way. As he went deeper and deeper into my love palace, I felt myself getting closer and closer to orgasm.

"Whose pussy is this?"

"It's yours, papi! It's yours!"

"Say my name. What's my name?"

"Dayvon, you big dick motherfucker! Damn, I love your ass so fuckin' much! Oh shit! I'm coming!"

As I was about to reach that ultimate point of no return, I was awakened by the sound of Malik's voice. I slowly opened my eyes and was startled by his presence. I was lying in the bed with nothing on but a thong; my hands were between my thighs, fondling my clit. Malik was pissed as hell to see me having so much fun in my sleep, thinking about another dude. In a fit of rage, he slapped me across the face. My head hit the headboard.

"Bitch, who the fuck was you dreaming about? It better not be that nigga who got your ass shot up," he said.

"No, baby. It was just a dream. It was just a dream. Why the fuck you had to hit me? Shit!" I yelled.

I was physically too weak to fight him because of my lingering injuries from the shooting. I had a permanent scar on my left temple where one of the bullets grazed my face. I also suffered nerve damage in my right arm. However, after going through extensive physical therapy over the last few months, I had regained some feeling and was on the way back to being at full strength.

The bullet lodged in my back caused severe pain that was unbearable at times. None of the painkillers the doctor prescribed gave me any relief. That was where Malik came into the picture. He had the right medication to take away all of my pain.

After he was released from jail, Malik went straight back out into the game. Over the last few years, he had become the biggest drug dealer in Brooklyn and was feared by everybody anywhere he went in New York City. When my mother told him about the shooting incident in Baltimore, he rushed down south to be by my side. In fact, he was the one who managed to get me outta the hospital before the police were able to question me. He whisked me back to New York, put me in an exclusive upstate hospital to get the best medical care, and paid all of my medical bills. Since I had been released from the hospital, he had been personally caring for me night and day.

The worst thing Malik had done was turn me on to one of the nasty habits he picked up in jail. Mailk had developed a heavy addiction to morphine. At first he used it just to pass the time while doing his bid, but then it became a daily habit. He knew its power as a painkiller, so when he saw me suffering, he gradually convinced me to try it, just to make it through the day. Seeing no other avenue to deal with my pain, I eventually gave in to him and tried it. I was hooked from my first blast. It was a marriage made in heaven.

Malik used my drug habit to control me. He knew I didn't love him anymore, but he knew that if he kept my ass as strung out as he was, then I would always be with him. He told me he had vowed the whole time he was locked up that he would get me back into his life one day by any means necessary, and I had fallen right into his trap.

My life, which had once been so structured and appeared to have so much promise, was in disarray. All my dreams and aspirations had gone out the window. I had constant nightmares about the tragic night of the shooting and seeing my best friend die right next to me. My heart was broken over losing Sasha and my one true love, Dayvon. I also couldn't erase the agony of losing my baby.

Physically, the wear and tear of my drug use was beginning to take its toll. It don't take long for a person with a dope habit to start to show the damage. I no longer cared about finishing school. My mother had to take custody of my son because I was neglecting him. Malik managed to get into my savings account and withdraw all of the money I had saved from dancing. Plus, he was riding around in my car like it was his own. My morphine habit had gotten so bad that I couldn't get outta the bed and function without a hit first thing in the morning. I didn't care about much of anything except getting high. I was becoming a zombie, tuned into channel zero. I was letting Malik and the drugs destroy me.

"Whatever, bitch. Since you been dreaming about getting some dick, I'ma give you just what you want," Malik said. He started taking off his clothes and made his way back over to the bed.

"Malik, please baby, don't do this. I swear I'll never do it again." I tried pleading with him.

Malik paid no mind to my cries for him to stop as he ripped off my thong and forced himself inside of me. I didn't have the strength to fight him off. Malik was about 6 feet 4 inches with a slender build, but he was strong. All I could do was lay there and take his pounding for twenty minutes until he reached his climax. My eyes filled with tears. What had I done to deserve this type of treatment? After he finished, he rolled over and looked at me with a sinister grin on his face. He didn't feel any guilt after just raping the mother of his son.

"Damn, that was good. Just like old times, huh, baby? Remember how we used to do it before I got locked up and you skipped town with my son?" He laughed out loud and reached over the side of the bed to retrieve a bundle of morphine he had for me. He set it on the bed next to me and picked up his clothes.

I didn't say a word as I watched him get dressed. I stared at him with thoughts of vengeance. I couldn't believe I had fallen for his nice guy routine.

When he came and got me outta the hospital in Baltimore, he filled me with a bunch of nonsense lies about wanting to be a family with me and li'l Malik. He told me he would never hurt me the way Dayvon did. I was in such a state of confusion over my feelings for Dayvon that I believed him. Never did I imagine he would do a 180-degree personality flip on me. He wanted to punish me for leaving him while he was locked down, and now he was doing a damn good job. He couldn't accept the fact that I had moved on with my life.

I was relieved when he finally walked out the front door. Now I was alone with my best friend. I laid out a few lines of the powdery substance on the mirror on my nightstand and inhaled them several times up each nostril. Once the morphine worked its magic, I laid my head back on the pillow and drifted off to sleep. I swore to myself this was gonna be the last time Malik would treat me this way. I knew who could fix this situation for me. If I wanted to escape this hell, I would have to make the phone call I had been trying not to make.

# 16
# Taking Care of Home

It had been almost a month since the last time I saw my baby sis, and I was starting to miss her spoiled ass. Being caught up in all this drama, I hadn't had much time to kick it with her. We normally got together at least once a week to do lunch or dinner. She would always hit me up for some money to go shopping or just to hang out with her girlfriends. I didn't mind giving it to her because I was so proud of my baby girl for all the positive things she was doing with her life.

Even though she had always been a straight-A student throughout high school, I still made her show me her grades in college to make sure she was handling her business and not partying too much. In her first year of college, she joined the AKA sorority to be a part of their social network. After I saw how fine them sistahs were, I made it my personal business to come up on Coppin State's campus on a regular basis just to check up on Kiera. She saw right through my schemes and told all of her sorority sisters I was off limits to them. She shoulda been ashamed for cock-blocking on her big brother.

I had arrived a little early for our dinner date at the Macaroni Grill so I got us a quiet table for two in the non-smoking section. I tipped the hostess a twenty to make sure she showed Kiera to the table where I was seated. As I was waiting, I decided to give Cheri a call. I hadn't spoken to her since this whole incident had jumped off. I would have to make a house call soon to make sure she maintained her position on my team. I fumbled through my speed dial list in my cell phone to find her number. It rang three times before she answered.

"What the fuck do you want, you no-good motherfucker?" she yelled.

"Damn, baby. You need to tone that down a notch. Why you bringing me the drama like that, ma? What the fuck is on your mind?" I shot back. Cheri had never come off at me like that before. I knew something had to be wrong.

"It damn sure ain't your black ass, you no-good son of a bitch. You need to learn to keep your dirty dick in your fucking pants."

"Bitch, for real, you need to check yourself. You really don't know who the fuck you talking to like that," I warned.

I was getting pissed as shit that she was trying to carry me like that. Her comment about my dirty dick had me wondering if she was trying to say I burnt her. I knew that couldn't be, because I ain't seen no pus-like shit leaking outta my dick. Then again, I knew I had been fucking Nikki raw, too, so I would have to go to the doctor to get that checked out, just for safekeeping. They say sometimes a dude can have the clap and show no symptoms. God, I hoped that wasn't true for me.

"Whatever, nigga. You need to be worried about yourself. You done fucked up my life, and I hope you get what you deserve for giving me this fucking virus."

"You are seriously bugging. I know I ain't seen you in a minute, but got-damn! How in the hell did I fuck up your life? You bein' really extra right now. If somebody gave you some virus, it damn sure ain't me," I said. In the back of my mind, I was bugging. I wasn't sure what to think. She must have been saying this shit just to get my attention. Could it be possible she was telling the truth?

"Look, Dayvon, I'ma keep this short. Don't call my house no fucking more. I don't wanna talk to you again. I want you outta my life. The last thing I got to say to you is that what goes around, comes around."

Before I could respond to her emotional tirade, she slammed the phone down in my ear. I tried to call her back, but she didn't answer the phone. I didn't know what done went down in her life to make her bug out like that, but fuck it. That was just one bitch I could cross off my list. I was getting tired of making that long trip to the ATL anyway. She just showed me how crazy she could act when she was deprived of some of this dick.

Find 'em, fuck 'em, and forget about 'em was all I could say about that situation. Outta sight, she would definitely be outta mind real soon. Nonetheless, I planned to make an appointment with my doctor the following week to make sure I ain't got the bug. My last HIV test was like three months before and it was negative. I wasn't due for another one for three more months, but I would have to do one sooner than that for safekeeping.

As I was trying to take my mind off Cheri's psychotic episode, I saw Kiera walking toward me. Damn, my little sister had grown up. She was fine as hell. She wasn't the pesky little girl who used to follow me around everywhere. She was a grown-ass woman about to do big things in this world.

She looked just like our mother used to look in the old pictures my pops had from when they first met. Kiera was statuesque, with long, jet-black hair that hung down to the small of her back. She looked like a young Beverly Johnson walking down the runway of some European fashion show. She had an athletic, sculpted figure from working out at the gym. Her honey-brown complexion complemented her almond-colored eyes. Her baby face gave her the appearance of an innocent little angel. That's what she would always be to me, no matter how old she was.

"What's up, mister manwhore?" she said. Kiera would always joke with me about me chasing pussy all the time.

"You better watch your mouth, girl. Don't make me have to put you over my knee," I responded.

"Whatever, Dayvon. You know I'm too grown for that," she said. She leaned down and gave me a hug and a kiss on the cheek.

"Yeah, yeah. So, tell me what's going on with you. You still seeing that dude, André?" I asked her. I was always up in her business about her love life. That's because none of these dudes out here were good enough for her in my eyes.

"Nah, we broke up a few weeks ago. You know how y'all brothas are when it comes to commitment. You wanna hit it and then forget it. Hint, hint."

"I don't know what you're trying to say with that last comment. I commit to *all* my women."

"Anyway, Day, I wanna know what's up with you. Why you been so secretive? Does it have anything to do with what happened to Gena?" she asked. She was trying to find out if I had anything to do with Gena's death since they were friends. She shoulda known me well enough to know I would never admit to anything like that, whether I did or didn't do it.

"Now, sis, you know you violating right now. I done told you about asking me about my business.

That ain't got nothing to do with you. You should just be glad you wasn't with her when that thing went down. I don't mean to trip on you. I just gotta straighten some things out, that's all," I responded, reminding her she was meddling in my affairs when it was best that she knew nothing. I always tried to shield her from the harsh side of my lifestyle, to protect her from seeing the street side of me. I was sorry she had to lose a friend, but shit, Gena had to get got, if not for principle, then just for spite.

"You know I worry about your crazy ass. I don't know why I love you so damn much," she said with that baby tone in her voice.

"Because I keep your ass dipped in Gucci, Prada, and all that other shit you like," I shot back, laughing.

She just smiled and said nothing. She knew her big brother took care of her. She also knew whatever pain she had over Gena's death was far outweighed by the fact that we were family and our blood bond was so much stronger than their friendship. That's why she dropped the subject.

The waitress came and took our orders. I ordered lasagna with fettuccine Alfredo on the side. She ordered chicken and shrimp over penne pasta with a spicy marinara sauce. Our food came out about twenty minutes later. We ate like two starving animals at the zoo. The food was good as hell. We both enjoyed every bite. After I paid the bill, we made our way out to the parking lot.

I looked around to make sure I saw Big Lou and Hank on their jobs, watching my baby girl. We headed toward the Acura TL I bought her the year before for her birthday. As we were walking, an old, black Honda Civic almost ran over my feet. I yelled a few choice curse words at the driver as he sped outta the parking lot.

"Look, I'm about to tell you some serious shit, so listen. I'ma send Pooh over to the house with some money to hold you over for a minute. Plus, my lawyer has an account set up for you to make sure you'll never have to want for anything in life. That's just in case anything happens to me. I'm into some real shit right now, but just know that big bro is always watching over you."

"I love you, Dayvon. When you talk like that you scare me."

Tears were glistening in her eyes. I gave her a big bear hug to let her know everything was gonna be all right, then told her not to worry about me. After we embraced, she got in her car and was on her way. Big Lou and Hank waited briefly before they left to follow her.

# 17
# Lettin' Off Some Steam

*The nerve of this asshole to call here like everything between us was all good and dandy,* Cheri thought after she hung up on Dayvon. Forget the fact that she hadn't heard from him in a long time, his promiscuity had totally altered the course of her life and forced her to reassess her future plans.

She lay on her bed and cried until her nose was running. She wished she could reach through the phone and strangle the life out of Dayvon for giving her HIV. At the same time, she was angry with herself for being so foolish to sleep with him unprotected. In this day and age, it was a well-known fact that HIV was the leading killer of Blacks in her age group. A woman with a college degree should have known better than to be so irresponsible in her actions.

Deep down inside, she knew she had to take an equal share of the blame for her situation, but her emotions wouldn't allow her. Sound, logical reasoning would lose out in this situation. She just wanted Dayvon to suffer for treating her like a fool.

Shit, if she had to suffer, she wanted him to suffer even more. That's why she didn't tell him she was pregnant. She didn't want him to know he had a child on the way. She was prepared to raise the child on her own. She knew how much he loved kids and not knowing about her pregnancy would fuck up his head if he ever did find out one day. This would be her little secret, one she took to the grave with her. If he did find out in the future, it wouldn't be from her.

After dealing with her emotions and coming to grips with the seriousness of her medical condition over the last month, she had decided to tell her family. Her mother and father were deeply saddened to see their child stricken with this dreadful disease, but they were very supportive of her every step. Her father wanted to find Dayvon and blow his brains out with a shotgun, but then he came to his senses. He realized his daughter needed him for support in this troubled time in her life, not only for her sake, but also for the sake of his grandchild.

Cheri's biggest concern at this point was taking care of herself and her unborn child. She took all of the medication prescribed by Dr. Day to keep her as healthy as possible. She wanted to insure that her baby wouldn't be born HIV positive. She had taken a month's leave of absence from her job, telling them she had unspecified family issues to resolve. She joined Bally's gym to get her body into tip-top shape. She became more conscious of what foods she ate.

Accepting the reality of her disease, Cheri had become determined not to let it defeat her or break her spirit. She swore to herself that she was going to be the best mother she could be, for as long as she was on this earth. With the support of her family and her faith in God, she knew everything would be all right. She wasn't gonna let a no-good man lead her down a reckless path of self-destruction like so many other women did.

# 18
# Good To Be Home

I had Dayvon right where I wanted him. He didn't have a clue it was me who sped by him in the parking lot of the Macaroni Grill last week. The tinted windows on the old Honda Civic and the fact that it was night didn't allow Dayvon an opportunity to get a good look at me. Besides, the Civic was one of the cars I used when I did my dirt, and Dayvon didn't know anything about it.

I had been following Kiera for the last few days, hoping she would lead me to Dayvon. My hunch paid off well when she met him for dinner that night. Now I would be able to keep tabs on Dayvon myself and find out where he was staying. After I sped outta the parking lot, I waited around the corner for Dayvon so I could follow him. I also noticed that Dayvon had Big Lou and Hank following Kiera for protection. I knew they were good at what they were doing, because I had trained them, but I was better. That was evident; they hadn't noticed me following them over the last few days.

I had been released from jail two months earlier than everyone had expected, due to over-crowding. The warden said they had to make room for the new crop of violent offenders recently convicted of charges like murder and rape. Fresh out of the joint, I had that hi-pro glow that showed I had taken care of myself while I was locked up. All those sit-ups and crunches had my abs as tight as a drum. The muscles in my arms and legs were cut like diamonds. I looked like one of those muscle-bound dudes in a fitness magazine. I shaved all the hair off my head and let my goatee grow in to give me a more serious, thugged-out look. Damn, it felt good to be home.

The first thing I did when I got home was stop by the crib I had shared with Gena to see the damage that was done. The house had been ransacked. All of my valuables—my TVs, DVD players, and stereo equipment—were missing. Of course I had heard about the robbery and Gena's murder while I was in jail, but seeing that damage myself made it all the more real, and it pissed me the fuck off.

When I went into the master bedroom, I noticed my hidden safe was hit. The safe was in the walk-in closet, but it was hidden behind the full-length mirror in a secret compartment I had specially designed. All of my money Gena had saved was gone.

Luckily, I had left my five vehicles at my Uncle Will's mansion out in Montgomery County. Will had agreed to take care of them for me while I was locked up. With all of my money gone, I would have to sell some of them to get back on my feet.

After finding out I had no home to go to, I went to the cemetery where Gena was buried, to pay my respects. Even though I was mad at her for fucking Dayvon behind my back, I couldn't deny that I still loved her. I convinced myself Dayvon had manipulated her into doing what she did, and it wasn't her fault. I would definitely make him pay dearly for that shit in due time.

Dayvon was supposed to be my son's godfather, but he left him out here in the world with no mother. That made me even madder. Luckily, Will took Manny in and agreed to be his guardian. He was the only member of my family or Gena's that Social Services could find. It was either my son stayed with Will or he would become a ward of the court and be forced to go from foster home to foster home. I knew Will would take good care of my son while I was gone. That was one less thing I had to worry about.

I couldn't go around any of the areas of the city where the DFL crew were, because Dayvon had things locked down. I didn't know who I could trust outta the crew. The DFL family I'd helped build was no longer my family.

I knew the perfect place where I could rest and get my thoughts together. There was a girl named Renée who used to visit me while I was locked up, and we had become pretty tight. I met her through my bunk buddy, Bashir, and we would write each other letters back and forth. I really didn't give a fuck about her; I only wrote her to pass the time during my bid. I was no different than most of the other cats I was locked up with. You see, nearly everyone with a little game in jail could find at least one woman who was so bored and depressed with her life that she resorted to becoming a pen pal for a dude who's locked up. It added a sense of adventure and excitement to her life that she wouldn't ordinarily have.

Renée wasn't a bad looking girl by a long shot. She stood about 5 feet 4 inches with shoulder length hair. Her chinky eyes made her look either Chinese or like she had smoked a lot of weed in her life. The latter scenario was likely the case. She had an average figure with medium-sized breasts and a nice firm ass that was just enough for a man to get two handfuls when he was banging her.

She came from a dysfunctional family. Her father and uncles molested her from the time she was six years old. She tried to tell her mother and her teachers in school about what was happening to her, but no one believed her and nothing was done. She wound up running away from home and had been on her own since she was fifteen. Even though she was a chronic weed head, she worked as a telemarketer for a credit card company. She was the type of woman who was just looking for a man to show her some form of positive affection to make her feel secure. For right now, I was gonna be the cat to do just that until I got myself back up on my feet.

# 19
# A Blast From the Past

Chauncey never forgot about the ass whipping that Ty gave him when they were locked up together. His vision was impaired for the rest of his life, as well as some of his motor skills, as a result of the beating. He refused to let this situation go away without getting at Ty. Nobody fucked with a South Side Killa nigga and got to live to talk about it. His family wouldn't have that shit in any way, shape, or form. He had to handle his business just to save face with his crew.

Chauncey got out of the joint about three weeks before Ty did and moved back to Philly. He kept tabs on Ty and knew when he was getting out too. Chauncey planned on making Ty pay for what he'd done. When he found out from one of his crew who was still locked down in Hagerstown that Ty had hit the streets, he made it his business to creep back down to Baltimore to find Ty.

When he got to Baltimore, he hooked up with some cats he knew from jail who hustled out in East Baltimore for Ice. They gave him the 411 on Ty and gave him some clues as to where Chauncey might find him. They also told him about Ty's beef with Dayvon. They suggested Dayvon might be a cat Chauncey would want to contact to get at Ty.

Nobody knew Ty better than Dayvon or had it in for him as bad as Chauncey did. They would be the perfect team to seek vengeance. Chauncey told himself he would definitely be in touch with Dayvon as soon as he got a little more comfortable on the B'more scene. Patience was a virtue, and he ain't have nothing but time to see his plan through to the end.

# 20
# In The Line Of Fire

My life was so fucked up I really didn't know what to do. My homey, Li'l Jay, was dead, Ty and Dayvon were both gunning for me, and to top it all off, I was looking at some major time with this murder charge. When Jay and I decided we were gonna go our separate ways so at least one of us had a chance to get out of this mess alive, that was the biggest mistake we had made by far. Since Dayvon got to his ass through that fucking freak, Bootsie, I had to deal with this situation all on my own.

I just escaped from Pooh's ass two weeks ago when he tried to bring me a move. Since I hadn't been around my old neighborhood in a minute, I didn't think anyone would notice when I slipped into the hood one night to check on my moms. I figured the police search for me had dropped off somewhat. My mother was real sick and dying from cancer. The doctor told her she didn't have much longer to live. I wanted to see her at least one last time before she passed away. With all the dirt I had done in my life and the pain I had caused her throughout the years, I owed her that much. She deserved to know I was alive. I wanted to spend some time with her so I would have no regrets after she was gone.

I just knew I would be safe in the neighborhood I grew up in, if nowhere else in this world. I always looked out for my neighbors whenever somebody needed some help with their bills or during Christmastime. I figured they would at least hold me down and not drop a dime on me to the cops or my enemies. Oh, how wrong I was. It's snitches everywhere you go. There's no moving about in this city without somebody seeing you. I was awakened to that reality one morning when I was on my way to the corner store.

I got up around 10:00 on that particular morning to go to the store to get something to eat at Corky's on 23rd and Howard Street. I placed my order over the phone. All I had to do was go pick it up. I ordered pancakes, sausage and eggs with cheese. Corky's had the best breakfast in town.

I walked up the street from my mother's house to the store. It seemed like an average day. I spoke to Mr. Johnson, my next door neighbor, as he sat on his porch reading the newspaper. Mr. Johnson was the eyes and ears of the hood. He saw everything that went down around the way. He told me that after the police first fingered me for the shooting, he would see them every day in their unmarked car on the corner, watching my mother's house. However, he said he hadn't seen them around lately. Feeling relieved, I made my way to the store to pick up my food. Little did I know his old, sneaky ass had set me up to take a fall.

After I picked up my food, I made my way up the block, back toward the house. I was startled by the sound of a car right behind me. When I turned around, there was a black Chevy Nova moving slowly toward me. I put my head down and pulled my hood over it as I started to run. The car picked up speed. Shots started coming toward me from the passenger's side window. One of the bullets hit me in the left shoulder and I fell to the ground.

As I lay on the ground, Pooh got outta the car with his gun drawn. As he got closer, he fired three more times at me from point blank range. All three bullets hit me in the stomach area. Before he could finish emptying the clip, I heard the sound of police sirens around us. Pooh raised his hands in the air and dropped his gun. I had never been so glad to see the police in my life.

When I was being taken away in the ambulance, I saw the police carting Pooh and Mike away in a paddy wagon. Turns out old Mr. Johnson had dropped a dime on me to the police. There was a $10,000 reward for information leading to my arrest. I found out later it was my old girl Tracy, who lived around the corner from my mother, who had tipped off Pooh. I had been betrayed by the people in my own damn neighborhood.

# 21
# Dishonor Before Death

Detective Warner and his partner, Detective Brock, were happier than two faggots in Boys' Town. The narcotics division had the DFL crew under investigation for several years, but they had yet to crack the inner workings of the organization. Sure, they had Ty locked up on a bullshit charge and he did a light sentence, thanks to Stink's help. They also got charges to stick on several lower level members of the team. However, that had failed to put a dent in the crew's control of the drug trade in West Baltimore. Dayvon kept the ship rolling smoothly, like it was no sweat that half of its leadership was locked up.

The information Stink had provided to get Ty locked up was helpful to them a few years ago, but this time they expected to get much more from their favorite snitch. Now that Stink's back was against the wall and he had no one else to turn to, they knew it was only a matter of time before he rolled over on Dayvon, Ty, and the entire organization. He was gonna be their ace in the hole to break up a major drug ring that had been a menace on the streets of Baltimore for nearly a decade. This would mean career advancement for both of them. They couldn't hold back their excitement as they made their way over to Union Memorial Hospital to take Stink into custody.

Luckily for Stink, two of the three shots he took to the abdomen traveled right through him, exiting through his back. They didn't damage any major internal organs along the way. The third one traveled through his body and lodged in his thigh. It wasn't a serious problem, so the doctor didn't remove it. The doctor was able to remove the bullet in his shoulder, but Stink would have to keep his arm in a sling for a few weeks.

Stink had lost a lot of blood from the shooting, so the doctor kept him in the hospital for two weeks. He wanted to make sure he didn't develop any type of infection from the surgery and there was no more internal bleeding. Stink was given heavy doses of morphine for his pain.

The whole time Stink was in the hospital, he was under police protection. They didn't want anything to happen to their star witness. As Detectives Warner and Brock made their way to interview Stink, they nodded and shook hands with the two officers posted outside his room. They entered the room and, without hesitation, got right to questioning Stink.

"So, Mr. Jackson, how's it hanging? I see you must have really pissed somebody off this time," Detective Brock said, calling Stink by his government name, Stuart Jackson.

Brock had known Stink since he was a kid. He had arrested him several times throughout the years. Along the way, they developed a mutually beneficial relationship. Stink gave him information, and he, in turn, made a few of Stink's arrests disappear.

"Yeah, they got me pretty bad. I'ma be a'ight, though. I know you gonna make sure of that, right?" Stink asked.

"That all depends on what you have to tell me when we go down to the station. We got two of your boys at the station now. We got them dead to right for the attempted murder charge on you, but that ain't enough. We want the big fish.

"You in some deep shit this time. Murder and attempted murder is nothing to sneeze at. You're facing life with no parole. Good ol' Jay got lucky and got himself killed so he wouldn't have to face the music," Brock said. He turned toward his partner and they both laughed. They knew about Stink and Jay's homosexual tendencies and how Jay was killed. They also had Bootsie in custody, and he was singing like a canary to save his own ass.

"Man, that shit ain't even funny. I'ma tell you what you wanna know, the whole ball of wax. Just get me the fuck outta here," Stink said.

Stink slid his jacket over his shoulders as he slowly raised up off the bed. He was on his way to the police station to sell his soul to the devil. He couldn't get mad at Mr. Johnson for selling him out, because he was about to do the same thing.

*A brotha gotta do what a brotha gotta do to survive. It's too late to turn back now. They say snitches get stitches in the streets, but I say fuck it. Sammy the Bull did it, and look at how he made out. The mob ain't got to him yet. Fuck Ty and Dayvon and the rest of them cats. I don't owe none of them shit,* he told himself.

# 22
# What We Do For Love

Walking back to my car, I was happy as hell. Things went exactly as I thought they would. After that crazy-ass conversation with Cheri a few weeks back, I made it my business to go to the doctor to get checked out. I decided to go to a free health clinic in Glen Burnie, Maryland, where no one would know who I was. They didn't ask me for ID, so I made up a fake name, John James. I told the doctor I found out my girlfriend was cheating on me with another dude. I told him I had unprotected sex with her and I wanted to be tested for HIV and any other STDs. I told him I didn't have any physical symptoms of the clap or anything else that I knew of. I just wanted to be sure everything was all right.

The doctor did a routine check of my genital area and said everything looked fine. He drew blood and sent it off to be tested. It would take about a week for the results to come back, so that was when I returned. I was relieved to find out my results were negative for both HIV and syphilis. The doctor warned me that I should start wearing condoms all the time from now on. I had to agree with him on that. Those hoes out there were scandalous.

He also stated I should get retested in three months to be sure everything was still okay. Three months from a person's last sexual encounter with an infected partner was the window of time the virus could lay dormant in the body without being detected. Little did the doctor know it had been at least three months since I had sex with Cheri. That meant I was straight. That psycho bitch Cheri surely got it twisted. She had better put that charge on another cat, because I wasn't the one.

As I rode down the highway, the DJ on the radio station was pumping the new DMX joint, "Where the Hood At." I was feeling that cut. X had a way of putting rage into a song that would make you wanna whip a nigga's ass just for G.P. While all these other cats spit all that bling-bling bullshit, always talking about how much money they holding and how many bitches they got, Pac and X gave that raw, uncut street shit the way it's supposed to be. Their message was clear and intelligent enough for even the square rap fan to relate to it. To me, their music was all about a thug nigga struggling, trying to make a change from the thug life, but the streets seemed to have a hold on his soul. I was definitely feeling that because I was going through that same struggle. I wanted to break free from this life, but it seemed like everywhere I turned there were more loose ends to tie up. I bobbed my head up and down to the track and let the chronic go to work to relax my mind.

I was caught up in my thoughts about Pooh and the amount of time that he was facing. I wished I never let him get involved with this game. I was supposed to be a father figure to him, but look what my guidance led him to do. Because of me, he was looking at spending the next twenty or so years behind bars. Yeah, he probably would still have a lot of life left to live when he got out, but he was gonna miss out on his best years. And for what? All the money in the world couldn't change the fact that the penitentiary was gonna be his home for a long time. I knew he would take his charge like a man and not mention my name or anybody else's, for that matter. The same held true for Mike. Nonetheless, that didn't ease my conscience, not one bit. I had to find a way to get to Stink's snitching ass. He was the only one who could connect me to anything. It was gonna be tough to get to him, though, because he was in protective custody. Notice I said tough, but not impossible. Time would tell.

I still couldn't believe that I was doing what I was about to do. Jaré called me a few days earlier and I damn near dropped the phone when I heard her voice. It was as though I had seen the ghost of

Pac or some shit. She totally caught me off guard. I knew it was only a matter of time before I heard from her, but I was still unprepared for it. I didn't know what to say, so I just listened. The things she was running down to me helped me understand what she had been going through since the shooting. She didn't sound like the confident, take-no-shit woman I knew. She sounded all frazzled, like her life was in disarray. Listening to her talk, I could see it was.

At first she was just crying and I couldn't understand what she was saying. I told her to calm down and relax, to run everything down to me slowly. She told me she was sorry for the things she said in her letter. She was just angry, which I understood. She said she loved me and always would. She ran down the whole scenario of how Malik got her out of the hospital and had been hiding her at his place in Brooklyn. She also told me about how he got her started getting high and she needed help to quit. She told me about his raping her several times and how he would physically abuse her almost daily.

I fought back my anger, trying to get the full picture. I couldn't get mad at her for getting back with Malik, since I forced her hand and pushed her outta my life. In the heat of confusion, we all do crazy things we regret.

She went on and on, telling me how her life was falling apart. She said I was the only one who could help her. After hearing all the changes she had been through over the last few months, I was mad at myself and ready to tear some shit up. I got her to give me their phone number and the address where they were staying. I convinced her to tell me where to find Malik so I could handle that problem for her, then I told her not to worry. I would take care of everything. That's why I hit the New Jersey Turnpike and headed north. My shorty needed me and I had to handle my business to make sure she was safe. She was my true love, and I couldn't fight it any longer. Even thugs need love.

I checked out Malik's little operation for a few days. I liked his setup and how he had his crew hustling hard to get that dough. I had to respect his gangster. Any nigga trying to get his weight up had to get his props. On the flip side, I'd seen him pistol-whip a couple of dudes in broad daylight, probably over a few pennies from a short package. That was totally stupid. That's just asking to draw attention to yourself. Plus, that's just setting yourself up to make more enemies than you need in your own camp. I always tried to handle that type of business in private, not for the public to see.

Sniffing all that blow must have been starting to fuck with his ability to think clearly. That's why he never saw me when I crept up on him on his way into the brownstone he shared with Jaré. The cold steel from my nickel-plated nine up against the side of his face woke him up real quick.

"Get your punk ass up them steps, nigga," I said as I stuck the barrel of my gun in the small of his back. I could tell he recognized my face, probably from Jaré's pictures of me.

He stuck his key in the door. We both walked up the stairs into the apartment. I called out to Jaré before I made my move, to make sure she was in the house alone. This nigga was about meet his maker.

"You know you ain't gonna get away with this shit. Something happens to me and my peoples is gonna be all over your ass, nigga," Malik said. He was trying to give me his tough guy routine, but I was hardly feeling it. I popped him upside his head with the butt of my gun, and he fell to the floor.

"Nigga, please. That's the least of my worries. By the time your people find your ass, we gonna be long gone. Hey, Jaré, you can come out now, baby."

As Jaré heard the commotion and made her way into the living room, I instantly noticed the change in her. The wear and tear of getting high was starting to show on her face. She had lost a lot of weight. Her eyes had bags under them and her hair was all over the place. I had never seen her look like this before. Even still, in her worst moment, the feelings I had for her made her the most beautiful woman in the world to me. When our eyes met, it was as though we were reading each other's thoughts. No words needed to be said. Our destiny was written in the stars. After I took care of this fool, nature would take its course for both of us.

"You set me up, bitch? After all I done did for you. You a ungrateful motherfucker. Remember that this the nigga that got you all shot up!" Malik said. He was making a plea for her to not let the inevitable go down. However, his arm just wasn't strong enough.

"Motherfucker, I should kill you myself for all of the shit you done did to me over the last few months—forcing your puny little dick in me, the way you slapped the shit outta me. Is that how you show me how much you love me? Is it? Answer me, motherfucker!"

Jaré was yelling at the top of her lungs. She attacked Malik, punching him as hard as she could in her weakened state. I pulled her off of him and held her in my arms. The whole time, I kept my gun focused on Malik, making sure he ain't try no slick shit. I gave the gun to Jaré to hold as I pulled the rope out of my bag. I sat him in a chair and tied his hands and feet. I made sure I didn't tie the rope tight enough to leave any marks on his arms.

"Come on, baby. Think about our son. We gonna get him back. Don't let him do this to me. I swear I'll never hit you again," he begged.

"I know you won't. Payback is a bitch, ain't it?" Jaré said with a sinister grin on her face. A burden would soon be lifted from her shoulders.

I went into my bag and pulled out the surprise I brought for Malik. Jaré told me Malik's addiction had gotten so bad that he started shooting up. She said he tried to get her to try it, but she refused. I got one of my workers to cook me up a potent hotshot of morphine mixed with battery acid. His death was gonna look like an accidental overdose. No one would suspect a thing; everybody knew he got high. They would just assume he got a hold of some bad shit and went out.

I cooked up the morphine and drew it up into the needle. I could see the life leaving Malik's body before I even injected him with the lethal dose. He was overcome with fear and unable to do anything to stop what was about to go down.

"Come on, dog, we ain't even got to go out like this. We two players out in these streets. Let's settle this like gentlemen. I got money. Don't do this, especially not over no dope fiend bitch."

Hearing them words outta his mouth did something to me. I said nothing. I just made my way over to him and tied a belt around his arm to find a vein. Once I found one, I slowly injected the morphine into his arm. His body started to twist and jerk instantly as the lethal injection spread through his bloodstream. As the hotshot took its effect, his body convulsions came to a halt. In a few minutes, he was deader than a doorknob.

After I checked his pulse to make sure he was dead, I untied him from the chair. I left the belt around his arm, as well as the needle in his vein, to make it look like he had injected the drugs himself. I told Jaré to leave most of her stuff in the apartment and only take what she needed, along with anything that could identify her. After we cleaned up the place, we were outta there.

Before I left B'more, I arranged for a cat I knew in Jersey, Manuel, to buy Jaré's car. Manuel was a crooked car dealer we used when we bought new whips. He had some kinda hookup at the shipyards where he could get luxury cars dirt cheap when they first came into the country. He was gonna pay fifteen grand cash for Jaré's car, no questions asked. He ran a chop shop and would sell the parts to make a nice profit. With Jaré's car gone, there was no more evidence of her ever being with Malik. It was gonna look like he was just another drug dealer who got strung out on his own supply. Keeping it real, he probably would have wound up killing himself anyway, messing with that dope. I just sped up the process.

We stayed in a hotel for a couple of days. Those few days were like hell. Jaré was going through withdrawal from the morphine. She was up all night, throwing up and going through cold sweats. Her bowels had broke several times. She was cursing and saying all kinds of crazy things I didn't understand, having hallucinations and talking about seeing pink elephants and shit. I swear I had to love this girl to go through all of this madness.

After about five days of her suffering, the morphine was outta her system. She no longer needed the drug to ease her pain. It seemed like just seeing me and having me back in her life was enough. I couldn't front, either, because I felt the same way. I was reconnected with my soul mate. This time, it was for good.

Our next move was for Jaré to regain custody of her son. I'd always had a good relationship with her moms before the shooting. She used to call me her son-in-law and say Jaré and I were meant for each other. I constantly denied it, but I guess Mother knows best. I had spoken to her a few days before I came to New York. I convinced her I was gonna take care of Jaré and it was safe for her to have Malik back. I told her Jaré was gonna go into a 28-day detox program to get clean. I had already set that up for her.

It took me a while to convince her mother, but she said if Jaré got herself together, then she would let her have custody of her son. I guess she knew that I would be a calming influence in her daughter's life. She never approved of my lifestyle, but she knew

I cared about her daughter. With that taken care of, Jaré and I made our way to Philly to the treatment center where she would be staying for a month.

# 23
# Hit 'Em Where It Hurts

The fresh smell of the Juniper Breeze candles filtered throughout the house and created a relaxed atmosphere. Kiera was home alone. Her parents had gone out of town on vacation. They would be gone for the next two weeks. That meant she was free to roam about the house, uninterrupted, to do as she pleased. There would be no nagging from her mother about cleaning up her room. Her father wouldn't be on her case about school and too much partying. Quiet moments like this were ideal for this young princess. She could enjoy the comforts of her palace in royal fashion.

The Freeman family had one of the largest estates in the Randallstown area. It consisted of six bedrooms and five and a half bathrooms. A classy, crystal chandelier hung from the ceiling in the dining room. All of Mrs. Freeman's glass figurines were on display in the curio. Full-sized mirrors lined the walls of the living room, full of Victorian furniture covered in the finest imported fabric. The floors were made of the most perfectly crafted marble.

There was a family room located in the basement, about as large as a medium-sized nightclub. This was where they usually entertained their company. It held a 60-inch plasma TV, a full bar, and a state of the art BOSE stereo system. There was also a Jacuzzi in the back.

Kiera was relaxing with a nice, long bubble bath. She was cleansing her silky smooth skin with a bath sponge as she listened to the neosoul grooves of Dwele and Urban Ave 31. She sipped a tall of glass of Chardonnay. Her mind had drifted off into her own private fantasy world. Her thoughts were overcome with images of her ex, Darryl. They had broken up when he went off to college two years earlier. Kiera was heartbroken when he left. She had dated other guys since then, but she couldn't seem to shake him totally.

He had called her the other day. Darryl wanted to get together to see if they might be able to rekindle their affair. Kiera couldn't wait for the chance to see him again.

Darryl was a tall glass of water Kiera liked to drink from to quench her sexual thirst. He knew how to stimulate her body to the point of unconsciousness. Darryl was about 6 feet tall with a slim, muscular physique. He had an earth-toned complexion with a set of piercing, dark brown eyes that made Kiera's pussy throb anytime he came around her. She loved running her fingers through his curly hair and kissing his cute dimples. Just thinking about massaging his strong, broad shoulders had her close to the point of ecstasy.

Kiera lifted her sponge and wrung out the warm water all over her supple, perfectly round breasts. Her nipples were primed for some major sucking at this point. She placed her hand in the water and pleasured herself in the way only she knew. Waves of pleasure flowed through her body. She made low, moaning sounds as her fantasy started to take on a life of its own.

"Oh, Darryl. Darryl. You feel soooo good," she moaned. She couldn't take it anymore. She released all of her pent-up passion at once.

Kiera was so caught up in her fantasy she didn't realize she was being watched. Her male admirer loved the view.

Kiera had forgotten to turn on the alarm when she came in the house. Ty had managed to sneak in undetected. Big Lou and Hank were no longer an obstacle to him getting at Kiera. Ty made sure of that when he put two dum-dum bullets in the backs of their heads. Their dead bodies rested outside peacefully.

"Damn, li'l sis, I ain't know you was such a freak," Ty said slyly to Kiera. She turned around in shock and covered her exposed breasts with her hands.

"Ty, what the hell are you doing here? How did you get into my house?" she asked. She felt both embarrassed and afraid that she was caught in this compromising position. She tried to act as calm as possible.

"In due time, baby girl. In due time all things will be revealed," he responded. He threw her a towel. The shiny black piece of steel in his hand told Kiera she was in danger.

Kiera stood and attempted to cover her body with the towel as she dried herself off. Ty had already seen what he needed to see. He was totally turned on from watching her play with herself. They say the eyes are the windows to the soul. Well, Ty's eyes revealed exactly what he was thinking. They were filled with nothing but lust and mischief.

Kiera knew she had to find a way out of this situation. She put on her robe and tried to remain calm. Ty ordered her to walk downstairs into the living room. He kept his gun on her the whole time.

"So, Ty, when did you get home? Does Dayvon know?" she asked. She was playing dumb, like she didn't know Dayvon and Ty were beefin'.

"Come on, shorty. You read the news. You know what's up. Don't try to play me for no fool. Where the hell is that bitch-ass brother of yours?" he asked.

"I don't know. I haven't spoken to him in weeks. Whatever is going on between the two of y'all ain't got nothing to do with me," Kiera said. Ty cocked his hand back and slapped her across the face.

"I ain't got no time for games. That nigga owe me. He killed my girl and he took my money. We got problems. Get his ass on the phone now!" Ty demanded. The tone of his voice frightened Kiera. She rubbed her face to lessen the pain from Ty's blow. She refused to let him see her cry.

"Gimme a minute. I gotta think of his cell phone number. Please don't hurt me, Ty. I'm sorry about Gena. She was my girl. I didn't know."

"Yeah, whatever. That's enough of the small talk. This is what I want you to do. Say exactly what I tell you to say. When your brother gets here, then we can finish the party," he said.

Ty ran the barrel of his gun along the edges of Kiera's robe. He was trying to get another peek at her breasts. He had wanted to get a piece of this fine, young, tender thing for a while now.

He ran down the script of what he wanted Kiera to say to Dayvon to lure him to the house. After she got it down pat, she picked up the phone and dialed Dayvon's number. Ty didn't know she called him on his business line.

When Dayvon answered, he instantly knew something was up. If Kiera called him on his business line, it was an emergency. Kiera told him everything Ty had instructed. Dayvon spoke in code to Kiera, in an effort to determine if Ty was there alone. He got as much information from her as he could without arousing Ty's suspicion, then assured her he was on his way. The waiting game now began.

# 24
# Judgment Day

Dayvon parked his Lexus around the corner from his parents' house in a secluded, wooded area. He turned off the engine and the lights, took his nine from under the seat and inserted the clip. He placed the loaded weapon into his dip.  He reached into his glove compartment, took out his shiny, nickel-plated .22 and placed it in his ankle holster. The second gun was his backup weapon, just in case things got outta control. It was small but effective enough to do some damage. He got out of the truck, armed for the confrontation, and crept toward the house.

Dayvon prayed Ty hadn't done any harm to his sister. She didn't deserve to be caught up in this madness. This beef was between him and Ty.  All of the drama he had lived out in the inner city streets was about to come full circle in the quiet suburbs from which he originated. What an ironic twist of fate this was.

Dayvon was glad his parents were out of town and not trapped up in the sick action movie Ty was directing. Dayvon knew Ty was a crazy motherfucker, capable of just about anything. Ty had nothing to lose at this point. Dayvon had taken away everything he had lived for. He got no more love out in the streets he had terrorized for so many years. All his money was gone. His woman was dead. Dayvon knew Ty smelled blood and was ready to tear some shit up. Nonetheless, Dayvon was prepared to give up his life if it meant saving Kiera's.

As Dayvon got closer to the house, he saw Big Lou and Hank's car sitting across the street. He didn't even walk toward it. He knew they were dead. He knew how Ty got down. Dayvon was sure he had taken care of them before he made a move on Kiera.

Dayvon checked around the perimeter of the house for any signs of Ty. The coast appeared to be clear as he made his way to the front door. He noticed all the lights were off, except for the living room.

The moment of truth was about to arrive. He and Ty would be face to face for the first time since their argument at the jail. So many lives had been lost or forever changed since that dreadful day.

As Dayvon was about to put his key in the door, he was knocked on the back of the head with the butt of Ty's gun. He hadn't noticed Ty hiding behind the large bush situated near the door. Ty dragged Dayvon's unconscious body into the house. The show was about to begin.

Dayvon was awakened by the force of Ty's hand slapping him repeatedly across his face. When he opened his eyes he was terrified by what he saw. Kiera was tied down on the dining room table with no clothes on. At that moment, he wanted to kill Ty with his bare hands, but the rope tied around his wrists had him bound to the chair and prevented him from doing anything. He knew what Ty had in store for her. It wouldn't be anything pretty. There was nothing he could do to stop him. Dayvon just hoped Chauncey had gotten his message in time.

Chauncey and Dayvon had hooked up a few weeks earlier after Chauncey reached out to him through Pooh. Seeing that they had a common enemy, they agreed to help each other out, in more ways than one. They agreed that whoever caught up with Ty first would let the other one know so they could share in the joy of getting rid of his ass. Chauncey also agreed to help Dayvon get out of town once all was said and done.

When Chauncey hadn't answered his cell phone, Dayvon left a message with the address to his parents' house, letting him know it was about to go down that night. Chauncey was the last hope either he or Kiera had of making it out of this mess alive.

"What's up, nigga? Where's all that mouth you had on the phone? All Billy Bad Ass and shit. Ain't got nothing to say now, do you?" Ty said to Dayvon.

He whacked Dayvon across the face several more times with his gun. Blood splattered all over his face.

"Fuck you, Ty. I ain't never want this shit. You set this off when you brought me a move, all over some shit that wasn't true from the jump," Dayvon responded. He was treated to several more sharp blows to the mid-section. Pain shot through his entire body.

"Don't bitch up, now. I had planned on getting rid of your punk ass anyway when I came home. I was getting tired of carrying your soft ass all these years," Ty said. This was news to Dayvon. His desire to get out of the game was just fuel for the fire that Ty already had in store for him. Before he had gone to see Ty at the jail, his life was already in danger. He just hadn't known it. The truth always comes to the light in due time.

"Yo, you can do what you want to me. Just let Kiki go. She ain't got nothing to do with this shit. She ain't never did shit to you. This is between us. Let's handle this like two street niggas," Dayvon pleaded.

"Nigga, please. Gena ain't have shit to do with this either. You took my money. You left my son out here on his own. It's funny when the tables are turned, ain't it?" Ty laughed in his face.

"I'm glad to see you brought the money. Now shut your fucking mouth. Sit back, relax, and enjoy the show. I'm done talking," Ty said.

Ty had instructed Kiera to have Dayvon bring two hundred grand in cash. It wasn't all the money that was stolen from his safe, but it was enough for him to do what he needed to do. He knew Dayvon wouldn't call the police because they were both wanted after Stink had dropped a dime on the entire organization. This beef was gonna be settled on Ty's terms. He was the judge, jury, and prosecutor. Dayvon's sentence was death, but first he was gonna be forced to watch his sister violated in the most degrading fashion.

When this was all over, Ty planned to move to another city and set up shop. He was married to the game for life. It was a vow he would not break until his death.

"Damn, Kiera. Look at how you done filled out. A phat ass, nice titties—I see you got the whole package. We gonna have a good time tonight. Smile for the camera," Ty said. He flicked the record button on the camcorder. He wanted to tape his performance and keep it as a prized trophy.

Ty put his pistol on the table and walked closer to Kiera. He placed his grimy hands all over her body, fondling her private parts. Feelings of disgust and shame blanketed Kiera's inner and outer being. She knew she was powerless. She tried to brace herself for the inevitable. Her body was paralyzed with fear. She wanted to cry out for help, but no words left her mouth. She prayed God would send an angel from above to save her. As it stood now, the devil had control of her fate.

Ty unzipped his pants and exposed his dick for her to view. He fondled himself in front of her until he reached his peak of arousal. He took off his shirt. Now he was naked for the camera to see. He used his tongue as a vicious weapon, assaulting Kiera's body. She cried as he violently sucked on her nipples and tried to stick his tongue into her mouth. When she refused to let him in, he punched her in the nose. Blood trickled down her nostrils. Ty aggressively pulled her legs apart and inserted himself inside of her. His brute force filled Kiera with sheer agony every time he shoved himself in. Her vaginal walls would never be the same.

The attack went on for about twenty minutes before Ty flipped Kiera over and began to fuck her up the ass with no Vaseline. Kiera had never had anal sex before, so the pain was unbearable. Too numb to yell, she cried silent, cold tears.

Ty was enjoying the rape and forcing Dayvon to watch. Occasionally, he would glance over at the camera and back to Dayvon, never saying a word. He was loving the fact that Dayvon could do nothing about what was going down. As Ty was about to reach his climax, he didn't notice the red dot pointed at his ass. A single shot was fired, tearing through his backside. Ty instantly fell to the floor.

"What the fuck!" Ty yelled. He tried to figure out where the shot had come from. It was Chauncey. He had arrived on the scene and peeped what was going on from the living room window. He had picked the lock on the back door and silently entered the house unnoticed.

"Brace yourself, nigga. Judgement day is here! Time to meet your maker, motherfucker!" Chauncey yelled. He let off two more shots, hitting Ty in both of his kneecaps. Ty's body jerked, and then he curled up into the fetal position. He was crying like a bitch.

"This nigga ain't as tough as he claim to be. Look at him. I've been waiting for this day for so long," Chauncey said. He kicked Ty in the groin several times to add insult to injury.

"Chauncey, fuck you. You wasn't talkin' shit when I was whippin' that ass over in the joint. I see you got some balls now with a gun in your hand," Ty said. Even though he was in a no-win situation, Ty was gonna go out like a soldier. Chauncey rained down on him with more blows. Ty couldn't move.

"Yo, fuck that nigga. Untie us, fool," Dayvon said.

Chauncey made his way over to Kiera and released her from bondage. She jumped off the table and headed toward Ty. She began kicking him with all her might as she relived the pain of what he had just done to her. She didn't care that she was standing there butt naked in front of a total stranger and her brother. All she wanted was Ty's ass in a sling.

Chauncey let her do her thing as he made his way over to untie Dayvon from the chair. He handed him Ty's gun. It was the same caliber as Chauncey's; this would work out perfect later when they made up a story for the police.

"Damn, nigga. What the hell took you so long?" Dayvon asked.

Dayvon's face was still stinging from Ty's assault. Without waiting for Chauncey's response, Dayvon grabbed Kiera off of Ty and embraced her. He got her robe from the sofa and covered her up, trying to console her as best he could. She cried in his arms and he cried with her. Dayvon knew she would be scarred for life. There was nothing he could do about it. He had to fix this situation somehow.

"I was tied up. I had to take care of some business. As soon as I got your message, I shot right over here. Better late than never. So, what you wanna do with this sorry motherfucker?" Chauncey asked. He had his gun pointed at Ty's head. He was waiting for Dayvon to give him the word to end Ty's existence on this earth.

Before Dayvon could answer, Kiera took the gun out of Chauncey's hand. Dayvon had no time to react as she emptied several rounds into Ty's body. His flesh now looked like Swiss cheese from all the bullet holes. He was dead. Kiera stood over him with the smoking gun in her hand. She managed to muster up the strength to speak.

"I don't know what came over me. Dayvon, what do I do? What do I do? Please fix this! You gotta fix this!" she yelled. She was hysterical.

"Calm down, baby girl. Big bro got you. I'ma take care of everything," Dayvon said with confidence. He was quick on his feet and knew just what to do. He had been in this type of situation before.

Dayvon instructed Chauncey to get his people to come and take care of Big Lou and Hank's bodies outside. He told him where to dump the car. Chauncey got on the phone to call his cleanup crew. They specialized in situations like this.

Next, Dayvon had Chauncey wipe all of his fingerprints off Ty's gun and anything he might have touched when he entered the house. He went to the camcorder, took the tape out, and put it in his bag. He would get rid of it later. He took the camcorder off the tripod and placed the equipment in the hall closet.

After that was done, he grabbed fifty grand out of the bag of money he had brought with him. He gave it to Chauncey. This was the money he owed him for his help. To Dayvon, this was a small price to pay for being rid of Ty. In turn, Chauncey handed Dayvon a large envelope containing the keys to his future. The contents assured his safe getaway, so he would never see the inside of a prison cell.

"It was a pleasure doing business with you, my brother," Chauncey said. He gave Dayvon a pound and walked out the front door. Like clockwork, Chauncey's people arrived and were already handlin' their business. These would be two dead bodies that would never be found. After they were done, they drove away from the scene as though nothing had happened.

Back in the house, Dayvon had calmed Kiera enough to run down the rest of his plan to her. He went upstairs to her room and retrieved a pair of her panties and a bra. He had her put them on then take them off so they would look like they were worn. He ripped them up to make it look as though Ty had done it. He gave her the story exactly how he wanted her to tell it to the police.

Dayvon instructed Kiera to tell the police that she was home alone when Ty broke into the house through the back door. Chauncey's forced entry was evidence of that. Next, she was supposed to vividly describe how he forced himself upon her. That would be easy for her to do, because that part was true. Then she would describe how she was able to wrestle his gun away from him. She would claim she blacked out as she began firing, as though she was having an out of body experience.

The bruises on her face and private area, as well as her ripped underwear, were compelling evidence in Kiera's favor. They justified her killing Ty out of fear for her life. Dayvon was sure the police would believe her. The case would never make it to court. A young college girl from an upstanding family attacked by a career criminal. What jury would convict her? Besides, Ty was a wanted man. The police would be glad to be rid of this menace. She might get a medal of honor or some shit for her bravery.

Kiera regained her composure as best she could. She picked up the phone and called the police, crying as she told her story. The police told her a car would soon be on the way. She hung up the phone and leaned over on the couch to lie across Dayvon's chest.

He had always been there for her in times of need. That was why she loved him so much. When their parents didn't understand, he always did. They sat and talked about good times. Dayvon was trying to take her mind off of things until the police arrived.

"I'm sorry you had to go through this, baby girl. If I could have done anything to prevent it, you know I would have. I would give my life for yours," he said. He knew she believed him, because he surely would.

"It's not your fault. I hope that bastard burns in hell," she said. She took another look at his dead body lying in the middle of the floor.

"He will, baby girl. Rest assured, he will. They got a gasoline suit waiting for him when he gets there," Dayvon replied. He heard the sounds of sirens getting closer. It was almost time for him to go.

"You know I gotta go, Ki. Handle your business. Remember what I told you. Big bro is always watching over you," he said.

Kiera didn't want him to leave, but she knew he had to. He was on the run and had to do what he had to do to stay alive. Dayvon gave her a bear hug. They expressed their love for each other then Dayvon headed out the back door like a thief in the night. He made his way through the woods in the back yard to get to his truck. When he got into his truck, he sped off down a side street, headed toward the highway. The police sirens echoed in the distance.

He knew Kiera would step up to the plate and handle hers with the police. She was his sister and he had trained her to be a soldier. Relieved that this chapter of his life was closed, Dayvon continued down the highway. He had a date with destiny that couldn't wait any longer.

# 25
# The Aftermath

The DFL crew was no more. The entire gang was broken up, thanks to Stink's loose tongue. What used to be a tightly knit and disciplined crew was now a scattered group of soldiers lacking direction. In the blink of an eye, all the strategic maneuvering and planning that made the DFL crew one of the most feared and respected crews in the city, by both the competition and the law, was undone by jealousy, envy, and greed. Every principle of proper street etiquette had been violated. Love had turned to hate. Murder had become the order of the day. No loyalty, honor, or respect existed among them. Ty and Dayvon's beef had affected the whole crew. They say when the head goes, the body will soon follow. Nothing was more fitting to describe the fall of this mighty empire.

Even though he gave up the entire organization, Stink was still sentenced to twenty-five years for the murder of Sasha and the attempted murder of Jaré. He would be eligible for parole in fifteen years. No drug-related charges were filed against him. He received this stiff sentence because he failed to deliver what the authorities wanted. He gave them the drugs, guns, and some money, but he failed to give them Dayvon and Ty. The local police and the DEA had wanted their heads on a platter, but Ty was dead and Dayvon was nowhere to be found. Stink's fate just went to show that disloyalty was never rewarded. He got exactly what he deserved for being a rat.

Pooh was sentenced to fifteen years for the attempted murder of Stink. The cops tried to pin Gena's murder on him, but they had no witnesses or evidence. Bootsie was supposed to testify to implicate him in Li'l Jay's murder, but he met with an unfortunate accident before he had a chance. His throat was slit and his face mutilated; his dead body was found in South Baltimore. Pooh would be eligible for parole in ten years. That was young enough for him to either start a new life or to wreak more havoc on the streets of Baltimore.

Shady Mike was given ten years for his involvement in Stink's shooting and for conspiracy to distribute cocaine. Tyrell was given twelve years for conspiracy to distribute cocaine and a handgun possession charge. He had a loaded .38 on him when he was arrested. Ronnie-O was given seven years for his charge. Shawn received the lightest sentence, five years, because it was his first offense.

All of them made out fairly well considering what they could have gotten, thanks to Mark Rubinstein. Dayvon had paid him well to make sure they all got off as lightly as possibly. Mark used his pull in the court system to make that happen.

With all of the majors leaders in the DFL crew no longer on the streets, their territories were open prey to any young cat who was creepin' on a come-up. The only thing that changed about the game was the faces of the players.

Kiera was never prosecuted for Ty's death. The police believed her story and called his death a justifiable homicide. However, the scars from her rape were evident. She started seeing a psychiatrist and attending a rape therapy group for support. She had to find some kind of outlet to deal with the perverted images of Ty that stained her brain. She was prescribed Paxil and Prozac to deal with her anxiety and depression. It would be a long time before she dated again.

One good thing that came out of this situation was the closer relationship she developed with her parents. She still longed for the day she would see her big brother again, but given the circumstances he would face if he came back to Baltimore, that seemed to be unlikely.

Cheri's life went through several dramatic changes. The HIV virus became undetectable in her bloodstream, and her T-cell count was back to normal, due to her medications, exercise regimen and new diet.

Much to her surprise, her ex-boyfriend, Larry, came to see her one day and dropped a bombshell on her. He admitted that he had broken up with her because he found out he was HIV positive. At first he hadn't planned on telling her, but then his conscience got the best of him.

Cheri had to eat some serious crow for accusing Dayvon of being the guilty party. Going further, she was still pregnant with his child, but she would never have a chance to tell him because he was nowhere to be found. Her child was probably gonna grow up never knowing his father, all because of a foolish misunderstanding. That was a burden she would have to carry for the rest of her life. She should never have jumped to conclusions before she knew all the facts, and now her mistakes would affect her child for life. Still, she felt lucky to be alive.

# Epilogue

Jaré looked as fine as the first day I met her. After coming outta detox, she was back to looking like her old self. Her complexion had come back and her body filled out. She had that junk in her trunk again and that glide back in her stride. She had surgery on her back to remove the bullet, and it relieved her pain tremendously. She no longer had an urge to get high. She had her son back, as well as the love of her life. As far as she was concerned, life couldn't have written a better script for her.

I observed Jaré from a distance as she bathed in the rays of the sun on the beach. The water was azure blue here in Cancun, where me and my new wife and stepson called home. I had plastic surgery in Europe that dramatically altered my appearance. That way I would be able to slip back into the States to see my family from time to time, once the smoke cleared.

My HIV scare taught me the error of my philandering ways, and I finally gave Jaré the commitment she had long desired from me. Thanks to Chauncey, we had new identities and a new lease on life.

I had wanted outta the game, and I got it in the end. I had truly paid the cost to be the boss. All of the time, energy and effort I had put into negativity could never be retrieved. I lost many friends along the way and took the lives of many innocent victims. All of the mental scars from my self-destructive life in the streets would forever haunt me. I would eternally be chased by my demons from living the thug life. I had wealth and a new life, but both me and Jaré were separated from our loved ones. We would forever live life on the run. In the end, was it all worth it? You be the judge.